PLANNING PENELOPE

ERIN LOCKWOOD

Visit my website at www.erinlockwood.com
Cover Designer: Phillip Lockwood
Editor: Madison Seidler, www.madisonsays.com
Proofreader and Formatter: Jovana Shirley, Unforeseen Editing,
www.unforeseenediting.com

This book is a work of fiction. Names, characters, places, and
incidents either are products of the author's imagination or are
used fictitiously. Any resemblance to actual persons, living or dead,
events, or locales is entirely coincidental.

ISBN-13: 978-0-692-88928-2

To my family.
You're my obsession.

ONE

She has an oral fixation, so I have an oral fixation—hers.

Usually, it's a pen cap, a pencil, or the plastic lid of her coffee cup, but tonight, she has nothing but her fingers lingering over her soft light-pink pout. I've been watching those lips and anything that comes near them for years now. It's more than my obsession. This woman has become my masterpiece, and I'm the unknown author.

I won't let anything chip away at my creation.

Especially *this guy*.

He's standing behind her, carnal determination obvious on his face and with a fierce urge to bite into the skin on her back. I can see it in his eyes, the way they're focused on her flesh. He leans forward, and my protective glands swell in my throat. Although I'm several feet away and one level down, I lean in, as he did, but with anticipation to lurch.

She's resting on the railing, staring out at the band onstage, unaware of what is about to hit her. Her left elbow is touching the metal bar, but her fingers are on her delicate, smooth pout, touching so lightly across, back and forth.

The loud nightclub drowns out one of her key senses. So, mine heighten in response.

I move to set down my beer. I'm ready. Ready to fight for her and keep her from the predator lurking at her back—the one fucking with my masterpiece. He moves closer to her skin and bends his head to kiss the top of her shoulder. She doesn't flinch.

I exhale a deep breath I didn't realize I was holding.

She turns around, wraps her arms around him, and kisses him on his mouth. Her delicate, smooth lips are on his unworthy mouth. My jaw muscles tighten, and my teeth clench. This makes me angry, but I won't act on it. Not yet.

"Alex, what's wrong?" Kevin asks, nudging me with his elbow, still keeping his beer close to his face.

"Nothing," I tell him and turn to pick up my beer from the high-top where I set it.

My eyes go back to her. They have been seeing each other for a few weeks, but I know it won't last much longer. Not after tomorrow. Not after what I found out. This one isn't the worst, but he's still not good enough.

Her typical type—blond, tall, fair-to-medium skin—Hitler's dream and my worst nightmare. I knew he would be a threat when they crossed paths last month. I keep them away as best I can, but there are too many unpredictable forces in life.

"Fuck, that chick is hot," Kevin says, nudging me again and pointing his elbow at a group of women dancing.

Keeping her in my peripheral, I scan the small group of dancers. I know exactly which girl he's talking about. "Tits are fake," I unapologetically inform him.

"Ass isn't," he quips. "Plus, who cares if the tits are fake? I don't care as long as they're there, and I get to put my face in them." I can see the wheels turning in his head. "I bet she has an awesome pussy, too."

I mentally roll my eyes at his distaste. "Don't forget about Michelle. She's not bad."

In fact, his girlfriend is really very nice—typical brown-haired, brown-eyed girl. Nothing like *her* but very likeable nonetheless. Kevin could do a lot worse—like the one he's drooling over.

He smiles at my compliment. "Thanks, man. I know how critical you are about women." His head moves back and forth to the familiar beat of the new song playing. "When was the last time you got laid?" he shouts over the music, forcing the conversation on me.

Last night.

"Is Michelle coming out tonight?" I ask, needing to change the subject.

"No." He tilts back his beer, taking the last sip the bottle has to offer. "She left to go home for Thanksgiving already. She wanted me to go with her"—he shakes his head wildly—"but no fucking way. I'm not ready for that shit. It's only been six months."

"You're right; she can do better." I pat him on the shoulder and reach my other hand across, offering to take his empty from him.

She and her tool-for-now boyfriend have shifted positions, and the crowd has changed now that more bodies have filtered in. I need to move as well.

Kevin follows me to the side bar. It's the one closest to *her*, where I can keep an eye on her while she's surrounded by predators.

"It's not that. I do want to be more serious but not yet. We're in our early twenties. We should be sowing our wild oats," he says, winking at his mediocre pick for the night.

She smiles back, and they know they can have each other, both at the tipping point. All that needs to happen is one move. But I need more time.

I grab Kevin by the arm to direct the few steps we need to make it to the bar. "Then, let Michelle be with someone else until you're done."

"No fucking way," he quickly says, picking up the pace and moving to the end of the bar.

I purposely take my position to face Kevin, where she can be seen over his left shoulder. I lean just in a way so that Kevin will think I'm making eye contact with him.

Two beats into a new song, and the crowd erupts, filling the room with sound in the absence of light. The dark club is barely recognizable, except for the small stage and the bar. I've always thought nightclubs were irresponsible for stripping young women of so many senses and topping them off with alcohol.

The atmosphere works to my advantage, making it easy for me to blend in. She never seems to notice me here. Just another face in the crowd. I'm careful, so she has never noticed me anywhere else either.

She loves this song. It's not her favorite, but I know she loves this song.

I watch her mouth move, and her lips form the words, *I love this song.*

I know the maximum distance I can be to still read her lips. From here, I can tell how fast she's breathing, based on the rise and fall of her chest. When I'm even closer, I can tell how fast her heart is beating, based on the shade of her blue veins and the color of her skin, combined with how fast and hard she's breathing.

"Coors," Kevin calls to the bartender. "What do you want?" he asks before the bartender turns away.

They both wait for my answer.

I take a quick look up to her. She's moving to the beat perfectly but too shy to be overly free with her body. He watches from behind her, looking down on her body, biting his lip, as if he were trying to hold something back.

If he only knew what *I* was holding back, he would run in the other direction.

"Nothing. I'm good," I say, pretending to look at Kevin.

"Nothing? You've only had one beer. Come on." He puts his hands up. "You're the one who invited me out. Get drunk with me tonight."

My eyes are still watching her, as I'm unconvinced she's completely out of danger yet. *He* certainly isn't easing my concern. "Not tonight."

"Well, fuck that. I'm getting drunk anyway."

"Go right ahead," I welcome.

Kevin drinks three beers during the time she has one vodka tonic. Now, the douche-bag guy she came in with is taking her by the hand and leading her toward the doors.

"I have to go to the bathroom," I tell Kevin.

He's still eyeing the desperation in a miniskirt with fake breasts. *Pathetic.*

"You'd better come back this time. You can't leave me here, waiting, like you did last week."

I walk away, not acknowledging his comment. Last week couldn't be helped. She was drunk. I had to make sure she got home safely and was left alone. It was a long night, but at least I knew she was okay.

"Wait, Alex!" he yells.

I turn my head in his direction.

"Are you always running off to get laid?"

Oh, for fuck's sake. Again, I ignore him.

"Wish *I* could get laid tonight," I hear him mumble behind me as I leave.

That asshole made me lose focus, and I've lost sight of her. I swallow hard and gather my thoughts for the best plan of action.

Without causing a scene or alarming anyone, I move as fast and as determined as I can toward the main exit.

I forcefully push my way through a cluster of people, nearly knocking over a petite blonde. I grab her shoulders, steadying her, as my feet keep moving. "I'm sorry," I say before she has a chance to complain about the run-in.

She looks up just as I'm releasing her, and any aggravation she might have had is gone.

"Wait," she asks when I don't stop to give her more apologies.

I have something important on my mind, and I don't have time for desperate women who will take whatever attention they can get. I have none to give. I let the blonde's voice fade into the background.

I step out in the fresh air, but there is nothing fresh about any air I don't share with her. Without moving my head, my eyes scan the area, looking for her. She's not out here. I dig my hand into my pocket, as if I were grabbing my car keys.

My white four-door sedan is parked in the side lot, but I walk toward the front lot, knowing where he parked earlier this evening. I get to the fourth from the left spot in the third row and stop. There it is—his stupid fucking Mustang.

I turn to head back inside. She'd better still be in there because, if he took her down some dark alley in the middle of the night, the only way *he* will be leaving that dark alley is in a body bag.

When I open the door to go back into the bar, I'm hit with a backdraft that ignites my senses with vanilla and violets. I step to the side, holding the door open for her to walk through. Her navy eyes glance up at me before she crosses the threshold. I force myself to look away from her and move my head back and forth just a bit, as if I were looking for someone already inside the bar. I move enough so that she can't focus on my face but not enough to draw attention to myself.

"Thank you."

I nod once without looking directly at her, accepting her sincerity as she passes.

Keeping her in my peripheral, I watch her silky strawberry-blonde hair move above her shoulders. Bunching it in her hands, she gives her lightly glistening neck the cool, fresh air it deserves. I breathe in, wanting to taste the salt of that sweet vanilla-and-violet-scented sweat.

He moves behind her, and I let the tinted pane close with me on the other side.

I lean against the wall just inside the entrance and look at my watch, as if I were waiting for someone. They stand on the curb, not moving toward his car, probably relying on the university-funded designated-driver program.

Three minutes later, a student DD's Prius pulls up, and they say their good-byes. She gets in. Only her. He walks off to his Mustang.

At least he had the decency to wait until she was in the car. Like I said, he's not the worst one.

Once both cars leave, I do the same. I know she's going back to her apartment. She studied all day, and she's ready, but she knows she still needs a good night's sleep before her test tomorrow morning. She'll get a ninety-two percent on her third midterm exam this week—Psychology 404. She does all the work herself. I just make sure she finds the right materials at the right time.

My BMW warms instantly after I start the engine. I will make sure she gets home okay, wait until the lights are out, and come back to the bar to apologize to Kevin. He'll probably be too drunk to notice how long I've been gone. Or better yet, he'll be distracted and off fucking some desperate piece of ass somewhere in that dirty club.

TWO

Penelope is inscribed with a black Sharpie on her paper coffee cup. She used to go to a dreadfully bad chain that was closer to campus, but during her sophomore year, I found a way to persuade her to Aroma—a locally owned establishment that imports all their beans from Italy and offers a French press with their table service. It's the freshest you can find in the greater Sacramento area.

Once I got her to take the first step in here, it took a lot of prep for her palate to make the change permanent. I injected bitters into her grape gum. When I knew she was out of gum, I went to the store she frequented ahead of her and injected it into the first pack. At first, it was a miniscule amount, almost unnoticeable. And then I increased the dosage over time, coaxing her tongue into accepting the strength of other pungent foods. Not only did I ready her for a change in her coffee venue, but she quit chewing gum as well. Once I stopped adding the bitters, she felt it was too sweet for her taste.

Then, all I had to do was set a small fire at the old establishment, so it would close for a few days, sending her straight to where I wanted her. It happened as planned. Always as planned.

Like her lips, her voice, and her body, her palate is delicate, and I knew how to manipulate it.

This cafe is quaint and personal. All the tables are different sizes and shapes—some round, some square—and none of the chairs match. It's about half of the size of the large chain down the road and about half of the wait time, too.

I still might be hiding my presence from her in here, but it feels more intimate, and I thrive on these moments. I make sure not to hold my paper too high, as to look suspicious, but not too low so that she could recognize me in another setting.

The penmanship on her cup is awful and doesn't do *Penelope* justice. It's the most beautiful name. Known for immense strength, intelligence, beauty, and—my favorite—faithfulness. She is all those things and more.

She always picks up the small cup wrapped in a cardboard sleeve with two hands.

I glance at my watch.

One, two, three.

Then, she brings the opening of the lid to her nose and inhales—*seven, eight*—and, now, she walks toward the door, holding the cup in her left hand—her dominant hand. Another one of her rarities.

Chills run through my body as I watch her nibble on the small opening. Just a little bite on the plastic before she tilts the cup enough for her first sip. She hums. But there's no time to sit and savor her coffee; she has a test to get to. She's on the move, and so am I.

I fold my paper and smile to the patron at the table next to me—something I've picked up from observing others. I grab my briefcase and walk out the door.

It's an extra three blocks to campus from where she used to go. Worth the wait and extra steps to watch the effects of Aroma's coffee. Her pupils change, her skin flushes, and even her breasts get perkier. She walks faster, and she smiles. All lips, no teeth. Her smile can brighten any darkness.

The sound of a softly playing guitar becomes louder as she nears the homeless street musician who has sat in the same spot every day since I first came to this university over seven years ago.

The guitar case is open, exposing the red velvet liner. She moves her crossbody satchel from her left hip to the front.

It's only seventy-seven cents. I've made a point to know everything about her—even the change she carries.

She always twitches a frown whenever she leaves less than a dollar. Pulling out all the loose change from her bag, she bends down and drops the coins into the guitar case.

And there it is—that little twitch the corner of her mouth makes when she wants to frown, but her face won't let her fully commit. She's too good for that in such a trivial moment.

Once I approach the homeless man, I contribute a quarter to his funds on her behalf. If she only knew it was more than a dollar today. But she can never know. Just like all the rest of them, I'm not worthy.

"Penelope," her friend Brandy calls out to her from across the street. She's balancing a dreadful cup of coffee in her hand.

Penelope waves and calls her over.

They have the same psychology midterm starting in twenty minutes.

Another student on the now-crowded sidewalk presses the crosswalk button. Twelve of us wait at the corner for that glowing man to appear to tell us it's safe to cross the street.

While I peer down at my notes, as if I were doing some last-minute cramming, two other people buffer the space between Penelope, her friend, and myself.

Penelope used to live alone, but I directed a drunk hobo to Brandy's apartment door last year. I convinced the mentally-challenged man that Jesus lived there, and she had to let him in. He was harmless, but Brandy didn't know that. Penelope was thoughtful enough to offer to share an apartment the following year. I knew she would after manipulating articles on the dangers of single women living alone to be in her line of sight. It's safer for them to be roommates.

I love the way their skin contrasts—Brandy, ebony and Penelope, porcelain.

"I don't know why you insist on waiting in those long lines. The time it takes me to walk three blocks to Aroma and three blocks back, you've been standing in line," Penelope's voice sings. "And," she adds with excitement, "it's better coffee."

Brandy crinkles her nose. "I don't know. I think their coffee is too strong. I'll only go there if I have to, like if *my* coffee shop has another kitchen fire like it did two years ago. I'm surprised you kept going to Aroma after the damage was fixed."

She shrugs. "I guess I just know what I like, and I like Aroma. I'm not going back," she says matter-of-factly.

In a mass group, we begin to walk. The skirt of her dress flows with each step she takes. The gray knit material is warm and thick enough to keep her fragile skin cozy in this late fall weather but comfortable enough for her long exam. She likes to readjust and cross her leg to the other side approximately every three to four minutes during tests.

I put away my notes and tuck them under my arm after beginning to walk across the street to the campus. Instead, I pull out my cell phone. It's a great way to keep her in my sights and convince people I have no interest in my surroundings. People may not believe in multitasking as much as I do, but everyone believes you can multitask while using your cell phone.

Her strawberry-blonde tresses bounce with her gait, her movements hypnotizing me. Fall, my favorite season, is the only time of year that honors her colors, highlighting her assets instead of blending in with the orange, red, and yellow. The colorful trees are like her throne, and she is the queen who sits upon them.

Penelope and Brandy reach the wide main entrance to the psychology hall. I bank a left and head for the back entrance to the adjacent building—the science hall.

I'll see you in sixty minutes.

I take the concrete and metal stairway to the basement level. I've reserved an hour of lab time every Tuesday and Thursday during Penelope's Psych 404 class—a course I completed during junior year of undergrad. It's during this time that I can do whatever I want within the lab walls. That's what over three hundred thousand dollars of private and government grant money toward genetic research will get you with a university like Tafford.

They should name the building after me—Alexander George Bishop V. But, to my delight, no such name...yet. Maybe after the award banquet next weekend. If I could avoid it, I would. But I think I'd draw more attention by not attending than the attention I'd receive when I go.

I use my set of keys to unlock the deadbolt on the thick metal door. The hall is lined with equally thick Plexiglas. Anybody can see me, but nobody knows what I do in here—not unless I want them to.

Once I flip the switch, the fluorescent lights flicker before fully committing to illuminating the room. I feel invincible in here. As if Clark Kent had taken off his glasses and ripped his shirt open to expose his Superman emblem on his chest. That's how I feel when I enter the lab. The research I've done and breakthroughs I've paved the way for is astounding. Even I know that. But nothing brings me more pleasure than my exploration of Penelope.

Setting down my notebook on the lab stool next to me, I reach into my back pocket and pull out a small plastic storage bag. I hold the clear plastic at eye-level and marvel at the one strand of brilliant strawberry-blonde hair, admiring the visible, perfect imperfections. It bends almost with the light but never gives in to a curl. Alone, it's a brilliant color, and collectively, they gather to form the same brilliant color. Most light-colored hairs have a transparency that changes in different light. Blonde, for example, will darken when gathered with more hair because it blocks the light from the pigment—or lack thereof. But this—I open the bag and pinch the middle of the strand with my thumb and pointer finger—has the same brilliance when alone and collected.

Every hair on her head is consistent. I've tested several of them. There is no irregularity in pigment, melanocytes, or cells. They are all exactly the same. Another oddity I can't stop obsessing over.

Her hair—it's what first drew me to her. When I saw her sitting in the library three years ago, I had never seen anything so mesmerizing. Her hair and the rare combination of her navy eyes took my breath away, and my obsession was born. I set out to know everything about her and her DNA.

I place it on top of a square plastic film, pinch a droplet of fluid, and add another square film on top, sandwiching my specimen. Moving it under the microscope, I peer through the eyepiece and begin to study my subject.

THREE

It's been forty-five minutes. I know Penelope doesn't need the full sixty to complete her midterm, so I pack up early. I have visions and longings to look at her full DNA profile today, but there isn't enough time during this lab session. That's something I enjoy doing at night while she sleeps when I can allow time to pass by effortlessly, marveling at her beautifully sculpted genetics and memorizing every molecule and nucleotide.

At one point, I almost hoped for a genetic disease that I would catch and cure for her. But, alas, that would not be my Penelope. She's perfect. My only plan is to keep her that way.

I place the strand of hair back in the bag I brought it in and bring it over to the lockers that line the back left wall of the lab. The lockers are meant for staff, but given they have offered—no, begged me to stay on for a full-time position once my PhD is complete, they've given me my own secure storage space. And a lot more than just storage space. I can basically do and have anything I want here. The university is my playground.

Passing the line of lab stools on my way out the door to lock up, I pick up the soft leather Brunello Cucinelli briefcase my father left for me last Christmas. Yes, left. It wasn't wrapped, and he was on business during winter break. But, nonetheless, I found it on my desk Christmas Eve. It means nothing to me. I wouldn't put it past him to have regifted it from some business associate of his.

Normally, I wouldn't have paid it any attention, except it's perfectly functional for what I need. Nothing flashy, just expensive leather and the right space for my research papers. And, no surprise, since it came from my father, it has a false bottom at the base of the bag.

I hope I timed it right. I believe I did. Penelope should be walking out of the psychology hall doors any moment now. I've seen the test, and I know she'll do well enough to feel good about her expected marks. Hoisting my right foot, I bend down and pretend to tie my sneaker on a cement bench.

There she is—the strawberry vision with pale skin—with her ebony friend, pushing open one side of the French glass doors to the fifty-year-old building. Penelope has what I like to call *my smile* on her face. I did that. I gave her that smile. It belongs to me, and in many ways, she belongs to me.

I don't bring my head fully upright until she passes and has her back to me. I'm about to take a step forward, but I freeze.

"Alex!" I hear Kevin yell behind me.

Fuck.

I hate this guy, but I need him as my wingman for nights when Penelope goes to the club. Kevin is easily controlled and manipulated. There is nothing suspicious about him wanting to go out drinking without his girlfriend any night of the week. And there is nothing suspicious about me ditching him when needed, so he can shag some whore or drink himself into a corner and piss on it.

The sound of his ex-frat-boy voice makes me cringe. But I need him.

I force a casual smile. "Kevin, hi."

We begin to walk in the same direction. I don't have Penelope and Brandy in my sights anymore, but I know exactly where she's going. The girls will part, but Penelope only has ninety minutes to pass before her next midterm. It's an easy course on nutrition she can do in her sleep. But, still, she'll make sure to be prepared and do last-minute refreshing in the library.

Plus, I need to cover my tracks after my disappearance from the club last night.

"So, what are you up to?" I ask as my icebreaker, pretending to feign interest.

His navy pullover, hiding most of his plaid shirt, and gray slacks tell me he was conducting a discussion group for his student-teacher position. But I don't typically see him at this day and hour.

"Midterm week," he begins to explain. "I told those jerks to study on their own before the test. Just handed them a study guide and told them to leave."

I nod as we continue to walk side by side.

"Good thing, too," Kevin continues. "I'm so fucking hungover."

Perfect. "Yeah, weird. I couldn't find you when I came back from the bathroom last night. I got another beer and waited, but then I eventually left."

Kevin smiles, likely thinking about his tired dick. I really hope he's using protection—at least with Michelle. She might be plain, but she doesn't deserve the diseases Kevin is probably carrying.

"Sorry, not sorry. That little number was just too hot to resist."

Wrong. But that's why Kevin is perfect for this position.

"Plus," he adds, "you were in the bathroom for a long time. I got bored. What the hell happened to you? Did you fall in or something?"

I shrug and look at him. "I guess that band is really popular. It was crowded. Long lines, you know." I've found that, if I ask him to agree with me, he always does.

"Oh, yeah. It was a crowded night," he agrees on cue.

We're almost to the library, so I reach into my back right pocket and pull out my phone. There's a text I need to send:

Professor Welt: Send the student I asked for to the library to drop off the documents I requested at study table seven.

Now, it's showtime. I bank a right, aiming for the steps between the guardian gargoyles perched on each side of the library doors.

"I've got research to do. I'll see you later, Kevin," I say as I near the steps to the water-stained gothic-looking entrance.

"Yeah, I'll ping you later. We can meet up again tonight," he yells out to me.

Nope. Penelope is leaving after her next exam, so I'll be leaving, too.

"Sorry, buddy, but I'm heading home today. Why don't you call the girl you were with last night?"

Kevin scrunches his face and looks around frantically, as if someone might be watching. He puts his finger to his mouth. "Shh," he says, taking a step in my direction. With a loud whisper, he says, "I can't bag the same girl twice. I can't risk Michelle finding out." He looks around one more time, just making sure the wrong person didn't catch on to our conversation.

I wish I could smile, watching him squirm, but I keep my game face on. "We'll meet up next week then."

Kevin is eager to accept my departure now, and we go our separate ways for the time being.

There is nothing like the smell of an old library. This building is about as ancient as the campus itself. It was the second building to be constructed almost one hundred twenty years ago when the university was first established. Now Tafford has grown to be the leading research university in the country.

The scent of new leather-bound books mixes with dust and chemicals used to preserve old documents. Between the books, newspaper archives, and articles collection, you can find almost anything you need to compete with the best of the best in academics.

Now, I need to find whom I'm looking for.

I walk down the long hall of tattered red carpet, passing rows of tall bookshelves on the first floor. My stride is not too fast, not too slow. I don't like to draw attention to myself, and I need to time everything perfectly.

As I pass the study hall, my line of sight grazes Penelope's beautiful profile, as she sits at a long table with an open textbook— her usual spot. I was hoping she would be sitting alone, and she is. Her eyes are deep in the book, unsuspecting of the bomb I'm about to drop on her.

Like other students who mill about the library, I walk on, passing the tables in the study hall, toward the private leased offices down the main corridor. When I reach room seventeen—mine—I open the door.

"So, I understand you'd like to earn points with your professor by helping me with a little research logging," I say as I cross the threshold. "Karen, is it?" I ask, never looking up at her. I keep my eyes on my desk as I unpack my briefcase and neatly place my papers where I want them.

She stands and extends her hand. "Yes, I'm Karen Schneider. I'm happy to help with whatever you need."

I eye her hand but don't shake it. I feel sorry for her and what she's been through. I might even feel a little guilt. She deserves better than to shake my hand. No doubt I'm opening recently carved wounds today—no pun intended—but I need her.

"You don't have to impress me. I'm not your professor. I'll only use you for the day."

She brings her hand down but seems nervous. Her fingers play with each other in front of her stomach. "Yeah, but...you're Alex Bishop. You're the one who discovered that gene editing could be possible with the right technology. You're the one—"

She tries to continue, but I really don't want to hear it.

I put my hand in the air. "That's enough. I know my credentials. You have a laptop?" I ask, stepping around the desk.

"Yes."

I hand her a flash drive with Tafford University and my initials inscribed on it. "Okay, then please log the research results from study Q27782Z44. You will find the data you need in section F, books 523.43 to 524.99"—I point toward Penelope's table—"right over there in the study hall section, right by table eight." I open the door for her to leave and play the part I need in this afternoon's show.

She reluctantly passes me. "Are-are you sure that's all you need? I can help—"

"That's all I need. It should only take an hour or two. Don't worry," I reassure her. "I'll make sure to let Professor Cunningham know how helpful you've been. You can leave the flash drive in my mailbox when you're done."

"Okay," she sighs.

I know she wants more. She's a budding genetic research pupil with a thirst for knowledge. Refreshing, but that's not what I need her for today.

She needs a little push.

"Now, go." I wave my hand back and forth. "Go, go, go, go, go," I encourage her to leave.

Karen does well. She sets her laptop at table eight, right next to Penelope, and disappears into the row of books where I directed her. I take my hiding place behind a vacant citation machine. I could easily look, as if I were searching old newspaper articles. Otherwise, I'm hidden and at a perfect distance where I can barely hear them. But, still, I read their lips for confirmation.

And, right on cue, the douche-bag-of-the-week boyfriend walks in with the research documents I requested from the bio science department. He smiles when he sees Penelope reading at her table. He needs to walk by her anyway, but now, he's walking toward her.

Penelope is unsuspecting, and his grin widens as he nears but quickly disappears when Karen reemerges from the bookshelves right behind my girl. They both stop in their tracks, and Penelope looks up from her book, suspecting there's something happening around her.

She smiles when she recognizes her new boyfriend. Her mouth opens to greet him with a hello, but the word never leaves her lips.

"Dave!" Karen screeches with a hint of whisper in there. She knows she needs to be quiet in the library, but how can she when she has a run-in with *him?*

Nerves ooze out of Dave's body. His eyes dart to Penelope and then back to his ex-girlfriend. "Ka-Karen, how are—"

"Save it, Dave." Tears well up in her eyes—the instant emotion I knew she would have when encountering him again.

Penelope turns to Karen and sees her distress. She looks back to Dave. "What's going on?" her voice sings.

And I know this will go down just as I planned.

FOUR

D ave looks down to Penelope with a pleading look, hoping for understanding in the explanation he won't be able to give to her right now. This moment is too intense, and it has nothing to do with Penelope. It's just necessary for her to be here to witness it and no doubt react.

"Karen," he calmly speaks, "I know you're upset, but can we talk in private? I just need to drop these documents at table seven."

Karen's expression doesn't change, and Penelope eyes them both with confusion and skepticism. She can't ignore the look on Karen's face and the obvious distress she's experiencing.

"Dave?" Penelope questions.

Dave's head moves slowly back and forth. He wants to look Penelope in the eyes, but he can't. He just stepped on a land mine, and he can't lift his foot—or his eyes—without detonating the bomb.

With his eyes still on Karen, Dave says, "Um, Pen, Karen is a friend of mine. I'm just gonna talk to her for a minute, okay?"

Karen sucks in a breath, as if she were punched in the gut. Her hands instinctively cover where she was hit.

Boom. The explosion I've been waiting for.

His words were cautious but not calculated enough.

Karen's face contorts, and her tears go from a light drizzle to a full-on downpour. "Friend!" she yells.

Dave cringes, knowing his mistake.

"Friend? You left me! You left me!" Her scream is loud enough for everyone in sight to look her way. So much for library silence.

Shushes come from a few hidden areas of the library. The students close enough to see are paused, watching it all go down, waiting to see what's next in this lovers' quarrel.

Dave pumps his hands up and down. His only movements because the rest of his body is paralyzed with just how bad this run-in is turning out to be. "Karen, calm down. I can explain."

Bang. Another detonation.

The dim lights and cathedral ceiling in this part of the library create the perfect setting for this scene. Their voices echo against the polished hardwood floor. A surround sound for my Penelope's beautiful ears.

"Calm down?" she yells, making the few nearby students flinch. She grabs her stomach again, drawing strength or memory, and looks around, figuring how many people are listening—the number of people to whom she's going to reveal her secret. "You had me abort our baby, and then you left me."

Penelope's lips make a wide O, and a gasp leaves her mouth. She looks at Dave in disgust. Just what I wanted.

Karen's body weakens after her confession, and Penelope looks up to her and debates if she should hug this stranger or yell at her now, at this very moment, ex-boyfriend.

She chooses the stranger.

The squeak of her chair scooting backward echoes throughout the study hall. She turns and wraps her arms around Karen, who instantly gives in to her embrace. "Oh my God, are you okay?" she asks.

Karen only sobs. Even if she wants to speak, she can't. All she can do is cry on Penelope's shoulder and fight for breath.

Dave takes a step toward them. "Pen, I can explain."

She whips her head around and snarls, ignoring the code of silence you're supposed to respect in the library study hall. "Dave, just go. Leave this poor girl alone."

A moment passes before Dave turns on his heel to set the documents down on the table next to him. Not table seven, but that's not important anyway.

"And, Dave," Penelope speaks again, prompting him to spin back around to face her one last time, "while you're at it, why don't you go ahead and leave me alone, too? I don't want anything to do with you."

The finality in her tone makes my groin ache. *That's right. That's my girl.* If I could stroke her gorgeous hair and pet her a congratulations, I would. But I keep my distance and get off, knowing I've once again sculpted another piece of her perfection.

Dave tilts his head. "Pen, Pen," he begs.

"No!" Penelope yells, igniting more shushes in her direction. "You stay the hell away. I mean it. Don't call, don't text, don't e-mail. Just get the hell out of my life. And the next time you see this poor girl again, walk away. She's better off without you, too."

"Pen," he tries one last time.

"NO!" she screams with so much force and assertion it could cause an earthquake inside my soul.

I love the sound.

Dave sheepishly turns his back on the girls, cursing to himself. *Bye, bye, douche bag.*

"I mean, the poor girl was devastated from the moment she saw him!" Penelope exclaims to her roommate.

I'm in my car at a nearby campus parking lot, listening. I can see the yellow glow from her window that faces Dalton Avenue.

Just watching wasn't enough. I planted bugs just before moving day. Usually, I just listen, like right now. Sometimes, I record. But that's only for very special moments.

I can feel her moving back and forth in her bedroom, gathering clothes to take home for the extended Thanksgiving weekend.

"Jeez," Brandy lets out. "So, did she really have an abortion?"

"Yes," Penelope quickly replies. "I sat with her for almost an hour, and she told me the whole story. I believe her. She wouldn't have made that up."

The girls take a moment to let the story sink in.

"I really feel sorry for her. I mean, she really thought he was into her. She thought they were in love. But, when she got pregnant, he pushed her to get an abortion and then split. He ignored her texts, calls, messages. Just left her high and dry. Who does that?" Penelope inhales deeply, adding, "She was so upset after seeing him. I barely made my midterm exam. I can't believe I ever went out with that guy."

I love how he has been demoted to *that guy*.

The simple metal frame on her double bed squeaks. No doubt her roommate is taking a seat next to her, as there's nowhere else to sit in her incredibly small room. Her double bed takes up almost the entire space, and she only has one tall dresser to store her clothes other than the narrow closet. She might have an extra inch if the walls weren't repainted over and over again just in this past decade. The place has changed hands, at best, once a year.

Her dresser holds only two framed photos. One is of her with her mom after high school graduation. My girl was valedictorian, top of her class. The other frame holds a picture of her and Brandy at a party their sophomore year. Other than that, there's no decor. She came here to study and have a little fun on the side. But she makes it clear that she's not going to waste her education at Tafford.

Brandy and her parents could have afforded a nicer or bigger apartment, but Penelope couldn't. She spent what little cash she might have had on buying her car last summer. She has survived here for over three years on her well-earned scholarship money. Something I admire greatly about her—her commitment to academics. Someday, she'll flourish financially, but for now, I love watching the way she moves through life like waves in the ocean. One of the few things I don't interject and pave for her. For now, at least. Until I see some sort of unfairness I need to correct.

Despite the monetary differences, Brandy was the best choice for a roommate. She's good for Penelope—as a friend and sounding board for necessary moments like this.

"Crazy how some things work out for a reason though. You were lucky to find this out now," Brandy tells her.

But I know better. Luck had nothing to do with it. It was me. All me.

"You've got some sort of guardian angel or something," Brandy adds.

Me. All me.

My jaw cracks as I move it from side to side, trying to relieve the tension. I feel a twinge to my ego. I want her to know it's me. But I can't. If I do that, it'll ruin my whole sculpture—the masterpiece I've been creating and been lucky enough to witness taking perfect shape.

I must see it.

She's become more than my obsession. She's become my way of life. I can't risk that being taken away from me. It's all I have.

"I don't know about a guardian angel," Penelope says. "I just don't understand why I can't find a decent guy. I think I've found someone worth dating, and then some horrible secret is revealed. Remember Jason? He failed a class and lost his scholarship after we dated for only a month."

That was my doing. I saw violent tendency and alcohol abuse in him. I wasn't going to give it enough time for her to see how far he might go with his unhealthy behavior.

Brandy sighs. "Don't worry. You'll find someone great. We both will."

I can feel the mood change in the room. This is why I like Brandy so much; she has the ability to keep Penelope up when she's down.

"Yeah, well, I hope it's sooner rather than later. I feel like I haven't had sex in a year."

Ten months actually.

They were beautiful episodes. I wanted her to have it. The wild, unbridled, passionate lovemaking. I needed to know what her moans sounded like. I only wish I could have seen her body and how it moved. I let it go on for four months, but good fucking was all he could offer her. He gave her what she needed—many orgasms—and then I found a way to send him off. He was kind to her but unmotivated and unworthy of such a creation.

I still listen to the audio I have of her coming. It's all I ever want to get off to.

An hour later, I see the bright lights of her ten-year-old red Prius illuminate in its assigned spot near the steps leading up to her apartment door. My car has been running this whole time, so all I need to do is turn my headlights on once I'm out of the parking lot and on Dalton Avenue.

FIVE

I never listen to music. The only joy it brings me is watching Penelope lost in the rhythm and beat of a song. Her movements delight me even more. The shy, small movements her hips and torso make when moved by music in public and the brazen and wild shadows that dance in her bedroom when she's alone.

I've thought about only her for the past two hours. No sound, no sunlight, just my thoughts of her. The way her breasts move when she breathes, the small, dark mole on her left collarbone—I love how it plays peekaboo with her spaghetti straps in the summer—the way her pen caps always transform into the same exact shape after one week of her nibbling on the tip, her natural scent of vanilla and violets. And, most of all, I think about her remarkable hair that can bring light to any darkness. Even the night's darkness on our way to her home in the Bay Area.

Driving from Sacramento to Berkeley is dull but familiar.

After unpacking her bag and laundry basket from the trunk of her car, she enters the apartment building her mom shares with her when she's visiting and disappears from my line of sight for the night.

Good night, my sweet Penelope.

"Hello, sir. Welcome back," greets me from the other side of the French doors to my parents' home in Atherton.

I didn't bother to park my car in the proper area but rather just left it in the circular driveway.

"Bethany." I nod to the house manager—my mother's trusted confidant and this decade's chew toy.

She means much more to my mother than just a manager.

I can't deny that her dirty-blonde hair pulled back into a low ponytail brings me comfort. She has worn her hair the same way for the past twelve years. Her mundane, blend-in-the-background clothing has been the same, too.

"You're working late. I assume that means my mother is here."

Bethany nods and moves out of the way for me to walk inside the home where I spent my childhood. I'm immediately greeted with the option of taking one of two winding staircases, leading to the floor where my bedroom is. I choose the one on the right.

The door closes behind me, and I can hear Bethany's flat shoes lightly tap on the foyer tiles.

"Would you like me to get your things from your car, Alexander?" she calls after me as my foot hits the first stair.

The sound of her voice makes me cringe. It reminds me of her intrusion into our family.

I barely move my head to the side as I continue forward. "You're my mother's errand girl, not mine."

I haven't brought anything but my briefcase, which is in my hand. My condo has a washer and dryer, so I'm not in the habit of bringing my dirty clothes home, like Penelope has been doing for the past three and a half years. Besides, I don't plan to spend much time here. As long as Penelope's plans don't change, I'll be back in Sacramento in three days.

My car is right where I left it—at the apex of the driveway, steps away from the front door. Bethany knows better than to have it moved. The grand awning and trees lining the property shade the morning sun from my eyes as I walk to my car. I haven't entered or exited this home any other way since I left almost eight years ago.

Just like all my other visits, the home is empty, except for my mother and Bethany. But that just means they're somewhere in the eleven thousand square feet. It's not as if my mother came looking for me last night after I arrived. She knew where to find me. I, on the other hand, wouldn't have the first clue on where to go looking for her. In her closet, sulking over what else to buy? In the wine cellar, drowning her sorrows? Or perhaps she was in bed, passed out after taking a sleeping pill?

I hear the call and feel the rolling in my abdomen. My stomach grumbles as I pull the seat belt across my torso. Driving back to Berkeley, I can stop at La Forine in Oakland and grab a pastry before following Penelope and her mother on their last-minute Thanksgiving grocery shopping.

The scent of citrus overwhelms me as I hover over the fresh produce. I see everything under the shadow of my Giants ball cap. It shades my face, and my loose clothing conceals most of my physical features.

Still, through all the citrus, I get a wisp of vanilla and violets when the air-conditioning hits her body just right.

"Mom, you look exhausted. We don't have to do the whole meal thing this year. We can just get something easy to heat up."

I noticed the bags under her mother's eyes almost immediately this morning. I've also observed the grayish tone in her skin. She's sleep-deprived and malnourished. But nothing unusual for a third-year med student. She spends more time studying than sleeping or eating.

"No," Penelope's mom argues. "My daughter is home for Thanksgiving, and I'm going to give her a proper meal." She reaches her arm up, caressing under Penelope's jaw and across her cheek. Her thumb moves up and down, soothing her daughter's skin. "I'm just so proud of you. You deserve a normal Thanksgiving dinner."

Penelope takes her mother's hand from her face and grabs the other. "Mom, I'm the one who is so proud of you. You're finally living your dream, and you're going to be a doctor. You inspire me."

They begin to walk along the dwindling grocery-store shelves. All the essentials for today's meal have been picked over. But, with her mom's busy class schedule, today is the only day for them to shop. They'll make do with boxed stuffing instead of from scratch since all the croutons are absent from the shelves. And they'll only be baking two large turkey breasts. It's too late in the game for them to venture cooking a whole bird.

I imagine they used to have a grand family meal every year. She used to be a stay-at-home mom until Penelope's father died when she was fourteen. They weren't left with much more than a mortgage. For some reason, her mother decided to pursue med school and obtain student loans. She would have been better off selling Avon items at this point in her life. But she hasn't burdened Penelope with her problems, and for that, I'm grateful I don't need to interject myself into her life as well.

"I think all we need are potatoes." Penelope leads her mom through the produce section.

I toss an orange in my basket and move to the back of the store. I peruse the nuts and dried fruit but have no intention of buying any. Once I know their shopping list is complete, I head to the far end aisle and begin checking out the four items in my basket.

I assumed Penelope and her mother would use the self-checkout or one of the other stalls near the exit closest to where they parked. But I assumed wrong. Their voices get louder, and I feel them near me with my back turned to the rest of the store.

"Mom, let me buy you a Vitaminwater."

"Well, if you really think I need it that bad."

The chill from the refrigerator shimmies down my spine. I remain calm and breathe evenly. *Don't panic. Stay in control.* The last thing I want is for her to recognize me here and familiarize herself with my face, only to expose my presence back on campus.

Beep, beep.

The sound of the codes being scanned could be the rhythm of my heartbeat. A pacemaker for the fragile position I'm in.

I twist my body to keep my face out of sight with my head down, my cap hiding my face as much as possible without looking suspicious.

"Not much of a Thanksgiving meal," the cashier says, trying to make small talk, while putting my items in a plastic bag.

I give a curt smile but refrain from speaking.

My credit card is shoved into the card reader. I'm just waiting to sign and leave as swiftly as possible.

Ah. The scent of her being so close crawls all over me, but I can't even turn around to see her. I'm overjoyed with the proximity but acutely aware of the danger.

And there it is—the signature line. I pick up the plastic stylus and scribble something completely illegible. Grabbing my plastic bag at the end of the cashier's stand, I walk swiftly out the door and into the parking lot to find my car a few rows down.

That was exhilarating but too close for comfort.

Following her home, I know this is the last time I'll probably see her until Saturday. There aren't any bugs in her mother's apartment, so I can't listen in. And there aren't any windows close enough to the streets to see her inside the apartment. They're on the fifteenth floor of the high-rise building.

I could try and break in to the office building across the street, but I'm starting to feel like I'm taking things too far. I'm feeling so desperate. The closer I get, the more I want to push the boundaries. My behavior is escalating, and nobody is more aware of it than I am.

Just because I'm drawn to it and I'm under some spell where I can't control my own actions anymore, I get out of my car and walk around the block to scout the possibility of entering the adjacent building.

SIX

It's taken me hours to mull over a plan. And I can do it. I can get into the building, and I can likely see into their living room window, possibly her mother's window. But not Penelope's. Her bedroom is a converted office in the interior of the unit. There are no windows in the room where she undresses and exposes herself.

Ultimately, I decide to go home—my parents' home. Penelope is safe in her building for the night, hopefully enjoying an edible meal with her mother. I will save the office-building plan for a more secure day when business is being conducted, and I'm at less risk of being caught violating the law.

The leather soles on my shoes squeak every couple of steps, echoing their scream in the foyer. The travertine has been polished recently, and the lack of friction catches on the patterned soles of my shoes.

"Alexander, is that you?" I hear the shrill voice of my mother call from the dining room.

I just wanted to grab a snack in the kitchen, not engage in conversation with my mother. In fact, I was hoping I would be able to avoid her my entire stay.

She calls again. I tread a little more carefully through the grand hall, past the formal dining room.

I'm almost in the clear and in the safety of the closed-off kitchen when a door swings open. Bethany's shoes don't make a sound. Years of mastering the skill of silence.

"Your mother would like you to join her," she says, nodding in the direction of the dining room.

"Would she?" I question. "Doesn't she have you to keep her company?"

"She would much rather see her son," Bethany speaks in a professional tone and clasps her fingers together in front of her, waiting for a response.

I move to take a step, but Bethany moves along with me, blocking my exit.

"Please, sir. Maybe if you indulge her this evening, she won't bother you the rest of your stay. Besides, there's already a place setting for you. Let's not have it go to waste."

I suppose there is a point in there somewhere. I was on my way to get a bite to eat. Maybe I'll kill two birds with one stone—scratch this itch my mother suddenly has to engage with me and eat some food.

"Fine."

My mother doesn't get up when we enter the wood-paneled dining room. I feel her smile graze me, but I try to ignore it.

Bethany moves to the seat at my mother's right and picks up her half-eaten plate of food, water crystal, and utensils. "I think I'll finish my meal in the other room."

"That'll be fine, Bethany," my mother answers.

"So sorry to have interrupted your date," I say with resentment.

They both ignore me.

The table seats twelve with my mother at the head of the long wooden antique piece of furniture. I scoot to the furthest chair away from the table and take a seat—my place setting, where she knows I'll be most comfortable.

As much as my mother tries to put off the inevitable, I can see the years accruing on her face. Filled with the latest age-defying trick, her skin stretches in an attempt to defy gravity. In my opinion, it's all for nothing. She used to be so beautiful, but now, she's merely holding on to something she isn't anymore.

Her unnaturally full lips move upward in an attempt to smile. But she doesn't try too hard. No, no. She wouldn't want to risk aiding a wrinkle by moving her mouth too much.

I do not return her lukewarm greeting.

"I'm so glad you're home, Alexander," she says as she moves her hand up to her chest in a sweeping, delicate motion.

The door to the kitchen swings open, and one of the staff delivers a plate of food covered by a metal dome to the setting in front of me. He removes the lid, and I can't deny that it smells good. I might be a little hungrier than I thought.

"I know it's not a traditional Thanksgiving meal, but I didn't know if you'd even be home"—her head tilts to the side, trying to look at me from a different angle—"or if you would even join me."

I eye the crab cake sitting on top of the saffron risotto as I pick up my fork.

"We never were the traditional kind of family, were we, Mother?" I'm hoping she read the undertone of my resentment.

The pain on her face is evident, but like her smile, she doesn't allow her face to move enough to loosen.

This conversation so far is painful, but this crab cake is delicious.

"So, Alexander, tell me about your experiments," she says with a genuinely interested tone.

It's insulting. She might actually care, but it is too little, too late.

I set down my fork and allow the clink it makes when it hits the plate to linger in the air for a moment. Dramatic effect. "My experiments?" I ask. "You say that as if I were a twelve-year-old creating a papier-mâché volcano for science class."

Her head moves back and forth, as she is desperately trying to find better footing in our conversation. "No, no, I didn't mean it like that. I'm just so proud of you. I know you've been doing great things at Tafford. I got an invitation for the dinner next weekend for the award you're to receive." Her breathing quickly picks up as she tries to get out, "I want to attend—"

My hand flies up in the air, and I motion for her to stop talking. "I do not want you there. There is no reason for you to go," I firmly state.

She takes an exasperated breath. "But, honey—"

I stand up, forcing my chair back. "Where is he?" I ask.

Mother pauses and purses her lips. She's trying to appear strong, but we both know she is weak.

I bend down and place my knuckles on the dining table. "I said, where is he?" There's a finality in my tone that tells her I'm halfway out the door.

Her eyes avert. "Madrid," she finally answers. "I think." She tries to feign casualness, but there is too much tension filling the room.

"With whom?" I quickly ask.

She looks down, ashamed. "Does it really matter, Alexander?" She whimpers, pleading me to stop my probing. Pleading for the topic to go away. Not just my questions, but also the fact that her husband has been unfaithful, likely the entire history of their marriage.

No. No, it doesn't matter. It matters that she ignores it. Don't ask; don't tell. What a farce.

"Sick fuck," I mumble under my breath, but the emptiness in the room carries my voice. I know my mother heard me. "I'm sure she's somebody so important, he can't even spend Thanksgiving with his family." Not that I care. I really don't give a fuck about either of them anymore.

She just sits there silently.

I've been here before. But, the last time, when I was eighteen, I walked in on my father screwing some whore. In our family home. While my *mother* was home. And, when I approached her—a scared young man, afraid he was going to break his mother's heart—I saw it on her face before she could even speak a word. She'd known. She'd known, and what was worse, she didn't care. She'd allowed it to happen under her own roof.

She began this meal without me, so she can finish it without me. I stand up, hold my head high, and begin walking toward the French doors.

The screech of her chair moving against the flooring is almost enough to turn my head. But I soldier on and keep moving toward my exit.

"If you hate your father so much, why are you so angry with me?" Her voice is as loud as I have ever heard it.

That makes me pause.

I place my hand on the doorknob. All it will take is a little pressure, and my escape will be staring me in the face. But there is one thing I need to say. "I hate you for putting up with it and enabling his philandering. If that upsets you, go cry on Bethany's shoulder."

Now, I press down on the handle. The door easily slides open, and I just as easily slide out of the room.

When I reach the top of the staircase, overlooking the garden, I realize the flowers are just about dead. How symbolic. There's no color where the row of poppies is typically planted every year.

I'll give just about anything to avoid seeing my mother for the rest of this holiday break.

I leave with the same thing I came with—my briefcase—and I book a hotel for two nights. I just hope Penelope keeps to her plans to return to Sacramento on Saturday. I don't like how I feel when I'm too far away from her when we're not on campus.

Back at school, I'm much happier, watching her shadow dance across the walls and play with the light in her bedroom window. I'm in my usual parking spot, and now that the U-Haul van has left the street in front of her apartment building, I have an unobstructed view.

Brandy is in there with her. The music is too loud for me to listen in on their conversations, so I'm just watching the carefree lightheartedness coming from her bedroom.

They're dancing, safe and having a good time.

After a stressful couple of days, I need to relieve some tension. Just watching Penelope doesn't seem to be enough. I need more.

My left hand reaches down beside my seat, finding the little lever that allows my seat to move back. I need as much legroom as possible. My eyes remain fixed on Penelope's window. I see movement in shadows, but every now and then, I see her beautiful hair flash its presence. The bounce and liveliness of it titillates my senses.

I unzip my jeans and place my hand in my pants, gripping my hard girth. Now, all my senses collide, and I don't take my eyes off Penelope's bedroom window. I feel as if I were touching her or she were touching me. We're one. And she doesn't even know who I am.

SEVEN

I'm woken up by a tapping on my car window. The sound of a police baton rhythmically beating brings me out of my sleep and into the conscious world.

Tap, tap, tap.

It's gentle enough not to break my window, but it serves its purpose.

The police officer scans the inside of my car with his skeptical eyes. In compliance, I roll down my window.

Morning sun screeches through the low-rise apartment complexes across the street. The rays move horizontally between the buildings. I ignore the shine and look to his badge to read his name.

Officer Smith uses his hand to shield the sun from his squinting eyes. "Overnight parking is not permitted," he says without offering eye contact.

No, he's too focused on finding something incriminating inside my car. My surveillance devices are in the hidden bottom of my briefcase. But things won't go that far this morning.

It was careless of me to have fallen asleep in my car, and I'm feeling less in control. But, now, I need to focus on Officer Smith.

"I'm sorry. I fell asleep while collecting data for my research last night." I look straight ahead, keeping Penelope's bedroom window in view, not giving him the respectful eye contact he denied me.

He clears his throat and grips his baton a little tighter. "What kind of research would require you to sit in a vacant campus parking lot on a Saturday night?"

He's itching for drama, but I take a bored-to-tears deep breath. "I'm collaborating with the neuroscience department on studies of female genomes and social behavior traits." I proceed to throw a bunch of big sciencey words his way.

I can tell by the way his pupils dilate, focusing on the stimulating words, that he's trying to figure out what the hell I'm talking about. A man with that posture, stature, and job choice likely has an ego. He won't want to admit his own intellectual shortcomings.

"Yeah, well, uh, I'm gonna need to see some identification," he says through my open window.

"Of course." I reach over to my briefcase and pull out my driver's license and a business card. "Here." I hand them both to Officer Smith. "Feel free to contact Dean Schumaker. He'll have no problem verifying my research."

He glances at my license and then fans the business card, as if it suddenly had weight he wanted to lift off it. "That won't be necessary. Just don't park here overnight anymore."

"No problem, Officer. Won't happen again," I say as I reach to roll up my window. Then, I pull the door handle and get out of the car.

Officer Smith swiftly spins around. "What are you doing? I just told you not to park here overnight."

I continue to walk off. "I won't. It's morning now. It's not forbidden to park here during the day, is it? Now that I've gotten a good night's sleep, I'm in the mood for a morning walk."

"Don't let me catch you loitering around here at night," he calls out to me.

I'm sure he's sulking that he hasn't caught a perp.

Not likely, I reassure myself. I need to be much more careful, and that's part of why I need some fresh air. I need to think.

I wanted so badly to touch Penelope last night. The urge is getting stronger. What started out as a mere curiosity has quickly escalated to a palpable need. Even more than touching her, I wanted to sleep in the same bed as her. I'm getting sloppy. Something needs to change.

The way I see it, losing control isn't an option.

I need to increase my surveillance to be closer to her, get rid of Brandy, find a way inside her apartment at night, drug her, and watch her sleep or, better yet, sleep next to her until the drugs wear off, slip out, and then let her go about her day as normal. I already have a copy of her apartment key.

Or I need to expose myself to her. Meet her. Actually meet her. Look into her eyes, possibly reach out, and run my fingers through her magical hair.

An irking sense of discomfort and rejection runs its course through my body. Bile rises inside me, and I feel myself physically shrink down. I shove my hands into my two front jean pockets, giving myself leverage to right my posture.

But then an idea hits me. *What if she doesn't find me completely repulsive?* In general, people have never found my looks repulsive. Forgettable maybe but not repulsive.

Nobody knows her better than I do. I know her preferred type, their style, their mannerisms. I can touch her the way I know she wants to be touched. *It could be me.*

It's so risky. I'm not sure it's the right plan. I need to calculate it more, analyze it, and make it foolproof.

I've only stalked around campus and the nightclub in casual clothing. I could clean myself up a bit. In my mind, I'm collecting the data I need to formulate a plan.

By now, I've traveled four blocks away from Penelope's apartment. I round the corner, and I am on my way back in her direction. I'm physically pulled toward her.

My ideas might have legs. I'll start working on the logistics and compare and contrast the possible outcomes in my favor.

As if the sun were on both sides of me, Penelope enters the street directly in front of my path, and the late-November warm rays beat down on my back. I feel as if I'd collided into a scenario I hadn't been prepared for. I'm rarely unprepared for anything. *Maybe it's a sign?*

One and a half blocks away, my feet keep moving in her direction. This could be kismet. My opportunity to test the waters and see how she reacts to my existence.

Alas, I have not showered in over twenty-four hours. I haven't changed my appearance or clothing, and most importantly, I haven't developed a calculated plan of how to approach her in the perfect way. If allowing her to meet me is the right choice, now is not the right time.

It's interesting to me that I'm toying with the idea. It's the first I've ever considered it in almost four years.

I reach the curb, only half a block from her body. All I would need to do is cross the street and bump into her in front of her mailbox on the corner. But I've already made up my mind. I cross to the opposite side of the street before she sees me.

Another man is walking toward the same mailbox, coming from the back end of her apartment complex. She doesn't see him coming around the corner.

I step behind a car discreetly parked in the shadows cast by the building adjacent to where she is. Penelope's head is down; she's playing with the keys on the ring she holds. There are only three keys on it, but it still takes her a moment to process and feel for the smallest one. She places the mailbox key between her thumb and pointer finger before she finally looks up.

The brick-for-brains man is about to collide with her while he's talking on his cell phone.

I want to warn her, but I don't think either of them is moving fast enough to cause any harm to her body.

It only takes a split second for her to realize the mistake, but the broad figure lurks over her delicate and perfectly proportioned body.

She bounces off his chest, as if it were a trampoline, and she squeaks out a scream, more from surprise than discomfort. The man drops his phone on contact and instinctively reaches his arm out to catch Penelope from falling.

"Gotcha," he says, holding her with one arm but then reaching with his other to bring her even more stability. His eyes are locked with hers, as if he were seeing some sort of miracle transpire right in front of his eyes.

It's just a beautiful woman. Get a grip, and move on.

If I had a dime for every man who showed interest in my Penelope's looks, I'd be richer than my father.

The problem is that my girl seems just as mesmerized as he does. But that doesn't make sense. This doofus has a jet-black mop where most of her beaus are blond and look like a perfectly put-together college Ken doll. This guy isn't even clean-shaven. The scruff on his face is trimmed. He actually wants that mess there. However, he does have the signature blue eyes she loves. They are bright enough for me to notice from across the street, but they don't hold a candle to the mysterious dark blue of hers.

Neither of them speaks at first until Penelope looks away due to discomfort or shyness.

"Oh no, your cell phone," she says, leaning down to pick it up for him.

"Oh, it's fine." He moves to pick it up himself.

Like coconuts bumping into each other, their heads clank. Both of their hands go to their own foreheads.

Penelope says, "Ouch," but shows no real pain. In fact, she's smiling.

Dark-haired boy just smiles back at her, allowing his cheeks to cave in at a very fine point.

This is a clusterfuck. It's hard to watch.

"I'm sorry," he finally offers.

"It's fine. Really, it's fine. I'm just worried I made you break your phone."

He bends down cautiously, gesturing for Penelope to hold off on trying to pick up his phone again. He flips it over and looks for damage but doesn't seem bothered by anything he sees. "Well, maybe I need to replace the screen." He holds it up to show Penelope the damage.

Her hand covers her open mouth. "I am so sorry…" Her voice trails off, and her hand moves forward with her palm open, searching for a name to call him.

"Nathan," he answers.

"Hi, Nathan. I'm Penelope."

Their hands meet between them, and again, they're touching, lingering on each other's skin too long.

It's only their fingers, I remind myself.

"Do you live here?" he asks, finally releasing her hand and looking up to the apartment complex next to them. "I just moved in last night."

A deep blush surfaces on Penelope's cheeks. I've rarely ever seen her in this form. I have never seen her have this kind of reaction with a first encounter with someone.

Maybe he makes her very uncomfortable, I try to convince myself.

"Yes, I do live here. Third floor, in the back corner." She points up to where her front door is.

This doesn't make sense. If she were uncomfortable, she wouldn't have told him exactly where she lived. She wouldn't be pointing to her fucking front door.

Nathan exposes his dimples when he smiles down at her. "I just moved here from being abroad in Italy last year."

Penelope's eyes widen, and she sucks in a breath, obviously impressed.

Big fucking deal. I've been to Italy dozens of times.

"I don't start classes until next semester. Maybe we can get together for a cup of coffee or something. You can fill me in on anything I might have missed last year."

Penelope tilts her head, hiding one of her blushing cheeks. "I'd love that. There's a really great Italian coffee shop I like."

No. No. No. That's our place.

"Great. I think my phone can still function. How about I get your phone number, and we can plan something soon?"

Her bottom lip catches between her teeth as she watches him hold his iPhone between them, ready for her number. "Of course."

Fuck.

They do what they obviously came there to do, collecting their mail from the mailbox. Penelope turns to leave toward the front of the building where she will take the outdoor stairs up to her apartment level. Nathan turns and walks toward the back of the building, the way he came. Neither of them can hide the smiles on their faces, even after walking away from each other.

Before she reaches the steps, she turns around and walks backward. "Again, I'm so sorry about your phone."

Nathan slows as he reaches the corner, not wanting to let her leave his sight. He flashes his dimples in her direction again. "Don't be. I'm not."

I can visibly see the heat course through her body. Her breathing picks up, and adrenaline allows her to fly up the steps, as if she were lighter than air.

This isn't good. For all I know, this Nathan guy could be a complete psychopath. Something about him makes me really uneasy. Angry even. This might turn into nothing. But, if it does, I need to dig up some dirt on this guy and get rid of him.

To hell if I'm going to let some sick fuck go anywhere near her.

EIGHT

I dragged Kevin out to the club last Sunday night. Michelle had even tagged along. It's a juvenile tradition to celebrate Sunday night before classes begin again. Just about everyone on campus was there with one pleasant exception. Nathan never showed up. All seemed calm, despite the large crowd. I didn't even have to make an excuse to leave Kevin and Michelle.

Penelope stayed for three drinks before she and Brandy shared a cab home. Luckily, since Michelle was with us, Kevin wasn't on the prowl and was happy to leave at the same time I convinced Michelle we'd had enough for the night.

It all worked out. Michelle might be an added asset since being in a relationship with her hasn't deterred Kevin from behaving like a single chump when she's not around.

Besides, I enjoy Michelle's company much more than her dickhead boyfriend's.

All week, I've had to listen to Penelope gush to Brandy about her run-in with Nathan. I know she's looking forward to her date tonight. I should be at home, working on my speech for tomorrow night's banquet dinner, but I can't miss this.

She also told Brandy how excited she was to have received a ninety-two percent on her psych exam. Just as I'd predicted. Her announcement was the most satisfying moment of my week so far.

My laptop sits open, blocking my face along with my hat. I lean across the uneven table to hide myself further behind my screen but to also tip the uneven table enough so that it won't shift every time I move—another flaw that adds to Aroma's charm.

We'll see if this boy really knows anything about Italy. They're due to meet here at seven sharp. I flip my wrist over and glance at my watch, only a few more minutes. I got here early to make sure I got the corner table in this small café. I ordered my favorite—a French press.

Ding.

My eyes flash up before focusing back on my computer screen. Nathan is here first. Out of the corner of my eye, I see him grab the front of his black leather jacket and adjust the material on his body, scanning the room for a strawberry-blonde beauty. His shoulder blades move up one at a time. It's a physiological reaction to stress—his tell. He's nervous about meeting with Penelope tonight.

I find this puzzling. Most men have a physical reaction to her beauty and enticing body, but Nathan's stress signs tell me he's emotionally vulnerable. Logically, it makes sense that an emotional reaction to someone would develop over time. He doesn't even know Penelope, not like I do. All he should know about her at this point are her physical assets. But his reaction tells me something different. This isn't physical; it's emotional.

Ding.

The chipped red door at the front of the shop swings open, and it's as if sunshine were pooling in the space around me.

I watch Nathan's face and body change when she walks through the door. I guess what he's experiencing is also physical because his muscles clench around his groin at the sight of her.

She sees him almost immediately and practically skips in his direction, her lower lip caught tightly between her teeth, keeping her from a broad smile I know she's trying to control. Her cheeks flush as she approaches him.

"Hi," she says and then reaches her arms up to embrace him.

"Hi," he returns, bending to wrap his arms around her back.

I watch him inhale deeply when her hair grazes the side of his jaw. He's experiencing the sweetness—exquisite, wistful, and powerful all at the same time, just like Penelope. I'd give almost anything to ensure my spot in place of his. If it were a monetary fix, I'd pay anything to have my arms wrapped around her body, so I could smell her fragrance straight off her skin.

Her breasts inflate against his chest, and her teeth dig in deeper to her bottom lip. Any more pressure, and I'd worry she'd puncture that delicate skin.

I hold my breath, waiting for them to part. For what feels like hours, they don't only touch each other; they consume each other with their embrace.

Finally, they part.

Penelope takes a breath and is the first to break the silence. "How is your phone? Fixed?"

"Fixed," he answers without removing his stare from her.

"I can't believe I haven't seen you until now. I thought I would maybe bump into you again this week," Penelope nervously says. She doesn't know him well enough to be relaxed.

His dimples cave in. "I was hoping we would, but I've been in and out a lot. I guess we just missed each other."

Their gazes hold on each other—again, for too long.

This time, Nathan speaks up to move the evening along, "Can I buy you some coffee? I know it's late in the day, but I love having an espresso in the evening."

"Right, you were in Italy for a year. I bet you drank espresso a lot over there," Penelope says with a whimsical song in her words. She practically hummed the word *Italy*.

He nods, smiling, likely reminiscing about his time spent overseas. "Every day."

They walk up to the counter together when the old-but-tireless owner stands to take their order.

"One espresso, please." Nathan turns to Penelope. "What would you like?"

"I'll have the same," she says to the owner before turning to look up at Nathan. "When in Rome, right?"

What?

She has never wanted espresso before. I have never seen her order anything but a cup of coffee. Once, she tried an Americano, but she didn't like it because it was too strong. She's not ready.

They collect their cups and take a seat, not far from me. It's a four-top, but they are sitting kitty-corner to each other. Their backs are to me, but I can hear them just fine.

Before braving her first sip, Penelope asks, "So, if classes don't start for you for another four weeks, why did you move in last weekend?"

"I did some traveling after my studies abroad in parts of France and Spain. But it was time for me to come home. Plus," he adds, "I've got plenty of credits to graduate at the end of the year

45

without the fall semester." He raises his eyebrows and explains further, "My parents don't live too far from campus. I thought it would be easier if I got an apartment rather than staying with them before school started again."

I hear a slight giggle come out of Penelope's mouth. "Easier for whom?"

"Me," Nathan answers quickly with a wry smile.

His elbow plants firmly on the tabletop as he takes his first sip of espresso, just skimming the beige foam on top.

Penelope follows his lead. I watch the side of her cheek to see if her mouth twists at the concentrated bitter taste of the shot. Like her date, she only skims the top of the foam and then sets down the small glass. Maybe I can't see her full reaction due to my angle, but she doesn't seem as bothered by the strength as I thought she would be.

"Really?" she says lightheartedly. "I would give anything to live with my mother."

"Well, it's not that I don't get along with my parents. I do. I was actually on the phone with my mom when I bumped into you."

Liar. He was probably on the phone with some other woman he's hiding.

Penelope's blush deepens at the memory of their first encounter.

He pauses and appreciates her reaction before continuing, "It's just that I've been on my own for a while now, and I'm pretty set in my ways. I'm not sure if I can go back to living under their roof."

"I guess I can understand that." She takes a subtle gulp before continuing, "My dad passed away when I was fourteen. After that, my mom and I really needed to depend on each other. I guess we still do even though we live a couple of hours away from each other."

I can hear the friction of leather and wood as I imagine Nathan's hand sliding across the table to reach Penelope's. I fight the urge to look at this moment, trying to avoid any attention in my direction.

"I'm sorry your dad died," Nathan says. There's a moment of silence before he speaks again, "So, you're *really* close with your mom?"

"She's my inspiration," Penelope says with a prideful, beaming voice.

"Tell me about her. What inspires you?"

Penelope breathes in slowly, as if she were smelling her coffee in the morning. "I don't know where to begin."

"How about the beginning?"

"Okay. Well, we were a happy little family. My parents wanted to have another baby, but for some reason, it just didn't happen. So, we were a happy family of just three. My mom stayed home because she wanted to make my dad happy. He never told her she couldn't work, but she knew that he would be happiest with a stay-at-home wife. She cooked, she cleaned, and she made my Halloween costumes every year. She was an incredible mom when I was growing up."

Penelope takes a moment, and Nathan waits patiently before she continues, "But then my dad died. I know it broke her heart. My heart was broken, too, but hers was different. It was devastating for her to lose the love of her life while I still had my life ahead of me. But my mom did the bravest thing I could have imagined. Instead of wallowing in self-pity and living out the rest of her life the way she had been living it before—but now alone—she picked herself up and created a new life.

"She's going to be a doctor." Penelope exudes excitement. "She used my last two years of high school to plan everything out financially. She prepared for the MCATs. Aced it! And then she got accepted into med school at Berkeley. And she's killing it." She beams with pride.

"That is incredible. I can see why you admire her so much. What does she want to practice?" I hear them both slurp a small sip of espresso. "My parents are both doctors, family practitioners."

"Really? That's great," Penelope says. "My mom wants to be a pediatrician."

"Look, I might not want to live with my parents, but they are great people, too. If your mom ever needs any advice or anything, I know my parents would be happy to help."

I peek my eyes just higher than my computer screen. Their espresso shots are still placed in front of them and are half-empty now. Penelope is keeping up with Nathan, sip for sip.

Her fair cheeks turn pink, and she looks down at the small glass in front of her. "That's really nice, but you don't even know me…or my mom, for that matter."

Exactly.

Nathan smiles at my shy girl. "Do you have to know someone to want to help them? I bet you help strangers all the time."

My thoughts go to the homeless man she gives all her change to before classes. And Karen—the stranger she recently defended against her boyfriend.

"Besides," Nathan goes on, "I want to change that. I think you're someone worth getting to know."

I look away several times, but I continue to focus on the glimpses I catch of them. They both lean in a little closer to each other. If this were the fourth or fifth date, now would be their cue to kiss, but that would be way too soon for Penelope.

"I want to know more about you, too," she says, looking into his blue eyes, only inches from hers.

Nathan grabs his dwindling cup of espresso and holds it up for Penelope to follow. "To getting to know each other," he says and then touches his mug to hers.

Their heads tilt back in unison, taking the last sip.

"Can I take you somewhere?" he asks.

"Now?" Penelope seems slightly surprised by his invitation.

He stands up and reaches his hand out for her to hold. "Yeah, I'm in the mood for something sweet."

Keep your fucking hands off my sweet Penelope.

"Okay." She practically giggles and gives her hand away to him.

As much as I want to dash out that door and follow them, I can't. I can't give away my position. Instead, I wait patiently as I watch them on the street through the glass windows.

They stand next to a motorcycle, parked next to the curb. *How the hell did I miss this?*

Nathan picks up a black helmet, the front covered by a tinted visor. They're both smiling and laughing while he holds it up.

I read his lips.

"Do you trust me?" he asks.

Her strawberry strands bouncing, she nods.

Why would you trust him? I want to scream at her.

With her answer, he holds the helmet in one hand and brushes her hair behind her shoulders with the other. He places the helmet over her sweet head before putting one on himself.

No. No. No. No. No. She's smarter than this. How can she be so stupid?

I start gathering my things, sliding my laptop into my briefcase. While my head is down, focusing on packing up and getting the hell out of this café, I hear the roar of his bike. I'm up on my feet just in time to see her bending over, getting on the back of the motorcycle, before she wraps her arms around Nathan.

They pull out just as I exit the old door to Aroma. They're off, but they won't get far.

NINE

didn't have to track her phone to find them.

At least he follows traffic signals. I didn't. I was able to catch up to them on L Street.

We pass by the prominent Capitol building while I tail them from almost a block back. Once I see him lean into the right-turn lane, I know exactly where he's taking her. There's not much open at this hour in Old Town Sacramento. Also, he said he needed something sweet.

There's no parking on the main street, so I pull into a diagonal spot around the corner. Still, I'm about a block away from Nathan and my girl. The old town is dying down with the darkening sky but still buzzing with some life from the tourists who haven't left yet.

Nathan and Penelope are walking away from Nathan's bike a half block away. They're coming toward me, so I pretend to search for something in my car until they pass and I can follow.

This part of Sacramento was preserved to appear untouched since the gold-rush days. It's a novelty tourists' love.

The loud sound of all the feet trekking on the wooden sidewalks drown out their conversation, so I have to listen very carefully in order to stay at a safe distance.

I walk steadily behind them as we pass the general store, moving with the crowd, unnoticed. Every now and then, I browse one of the shop windows to appear touristy.

I like her so much better without that black mass stuck over her head. She shouldn't be riding on something so dangerous. I've never seen her behave so spontaneously. Looking at her now, you'd never know she was riding up to forty miles per hour with unkempt hair. She looks as lovely as if she had just brushed it one hundred times with boar's hair bristles. Just like I used to watch my mother do when I was a boy.

"Have you eaten yet?" Nathan asks her and purposely swings his hand so that the back of it brushes against hers.

Penelope nods. "I had a sandwich after my last class, so I'm not terribly hungry." She winces. "I thought we were just meeting for coffee, so I made sure to eat before we met."

His arm reaches over and lightly touches her elbow. It slides down her arm, and their fingers instinctively intertwine once he reaches her palm.

"We just *started* with coffee," he says. He yanks on her arm, bringing her with him into the candy shop—one of the few stores on the old town block that stays open until ten.

Hundreds of large, identical barrels line up to create aisles of endless candy. All colors of the rainbow can be found in here.

"I've never seen so much candy in my life!" she exclaims.

They start to walk down the middle aisle, but I stay outside for a moment, giving them enough space to think they're alone. But I would never leave her alone.

Nathan looks at her, amused. "You're telling me that you've been going to school here for nearly four years, and you've never been to The Candy Barrel?"

I step into the store, perusing some of the treats in baskets on the shelves. Little pieces of caramel and candy I haven't seen in decades.

Penelope shrugs and shakes her head. "I've been pretty focused on school. I don't think I've ever left campus other than to go to the club."

"Ah, the club." Nathan grabs a cellophane bag from the end of the first aisle. He picks up a few candies in one of the barrels and drops it in the bag. "I haven't been for over a year. Maybe you can take me this week?"

They stop walking and face each other, and Nathan unwraps a candy in his hand.

"I don't think you're supposed to eat the candy before you pay for it. Wouldn't that be stealing?"

He pulls the piece of taffy out of the wax paper and holds it between his thumb and index finger. "Are you worried that you're on a date with a thief?" he asks, holding the candy a little higher and closer to her mouth.

Her inhale when he mentioned the word *date* tells me the idea excites her. Her feelings are on the edge of danger when she's around this man.

He slowly moves the taffy closer to her beautiful, pink pout, and her mouth opens as it nears. Although he's moving and she's reacting, neither one of them breaks eye contact.

The candy brushes past her lips, and she bites down once it's halfway in. Her teeth easily move through the soft, sugary bite, nearly missing his fingers. But her lips don't. Nathan pulls the candy away from her and places the remaining bite in his own mouth. His tongue subtly, almost unnoticeably—but I notice— reaches out to his fingers. The ones that were just touching Penelope's lips. He secretly tastes her.

I can't take this horseshit any longer. As I walk by it, I pull one of the legs on a tripod holding up a small barrel of gumballs. It takes just enough time to tip over for me to escape into another section of the store. The gumballs come crashing down, and everyone's heads turn to see nobody near the fallen candy. Nathan and Penelope become onlookers as the employees rush to clean up the bouncing mess.

"Don't worry; we'll take care of this," says a man in a white-and-red-striped shirt.

They see the cleanup is in good hands, so they move about the store. Nathan picks up a few candies every now and then and adds it to his collection. Once they've seen just about every treat in the store and discussed all their favorite childhood candies, they stand in the checkout line and wait to pay.

There are carousel horses leading up to the cash registers.

Penelope grabs on to one of the shiny gold bars and swings her body around to face Nathan. "So, you seem kind, generous, smart, and..."

She doesn't finish her sentence, but they both know what she's trying to say. She licks her lips as her eyes mull over his face and upper body. She's sexually attracted to him.

"Not bad-looking," she teases. "Well, you just seem like the whole package. Why are you single?" She bows her head with a blush when she sees his dimples. "You are single, right?" she adds in a panic.

He smiles at her playfully and shakes his head, making a strand of hair fly back to where it's supposed to be. "Yes," he answers and then adds, "I'm flattered by the implication of your question." He tries not to smile too broadly, so he purses his lips quickly to reset. "But I just got back in town. What's your excuse?"

They move up in the short line.

"Why isn't someone bending over backward to keep you?" he asks his question in another way.

I am. I'm bending over backward to keep her.

Penelope takes a deep breath, and her eyes flutter up to the left corner. "I don't know. Relationships just haven't worked out for me. I had a steady boyfriend in high school, but that was just puppy love. I've had one bad seed after another since I've been at Tafford. Maybe there's something in the water." She tries to exhale a lighthearted laugh and looks away.

The line moves again, so Penelope takes another step forward.

Nathan's eyes have never left her after her admission. He jumps in front of her, making her step into his chest. "Or," he says, "maybe you just haven't bumped into the right person yet."

"Next," the teller calls and waves them forward.

The moving moment Nathan was trying to force quickly dissipates as they move up to the cash register.

I put the bag of candy I was collecting on a random shelf and walk out the door ahead of them. I wait on the other side of the window, pretending to read an ad stapled to the frame.

Nathan pays for the bag of candy, plus one more. He didn't let Penelope steal a bite of taffy after all.

They walk around for another hour, chatting and eating their sweets. So, I walk around. Most of their conversation is small talk about their childhoods. Nathan has one sister, younger, but he doesn't share how old. He exposes little more about himself than the most normal upbringing. He could be lying, but soon, I'll know everything there is to know. I'll find every bad deed he's ever done, and I'll expose him for the fraud that he is.

Penelope tells him that she's a psychology major, and he reveals that he's majoring in international studies. I don't have any contacts in that department, but I'll figure something out.

There were a few times when Penelope laughed and opened the sky. The sound is equal to an angel playing a harp. It's the most beautiful sound I've ever heard.

What I don't like is the way her body reacts to his. Her physiological signs are telling me he's different from the other men she's encountered. She doesn't know what she's doing, and I must protect her.

Once he drives her home on his motorcycle, Nathan parks his bike in the back lot, adjacent to Dalton Street, closer to the entrance he uses to reach his unit. After removing their helmets and securing them on his bike, he walks her around to the stairway leading up to Penelope's apartment. The one I love to watch her in.

I'm parked on Dalton Street, just a few rows of cars back. The lights in my car are off, and I'm leaning far back in my seat. For all they know, this is just another empty car on the side of the road.

When they round the corner where the mailbox is, they stop.

I read Nathan's lips as they move to speak with Penelope.

"This is where we first met," he says with a whimsical look on his face, as if he were somewhere off in the clouds.

His mouth turns into a wry smile, exposing his dimples, and I know what he's thinking. He's hoping for a kiss. But he doesn't know my girl. My girl would never kiss on the first date. She never has, and she never will—not if I can help it.

Penelope nods and releases the most harmonious sound from the most beautiful soul—a giggle. He can do that. He can let her laugh, so I can hear that wonderful sound. I'm almost appreciative.

She's not trying to hide her blush anymore. Her cheeks puff and fill with rosiness, and her eyes shine up to him. Her deep navy pools illuminate light in his direction. She's begging him for more attention.

"I hope I bump into you again soon," Nathan says, becoming more serious with his gaze.

Enough with the bumping-into-each-other puns.

His hands twitch at the desire to reach out and touch her. But they remain at his side.

The still of the night mocks them as they stand there, motionless, speechless—just standing and staring at each other. I'm getting bored, having to witness this awkwardness.

"Good night," Penelope finally says, cutting into the silence.

She turns to leave him and takes a step in the opposite direction, but he catches her hand. He yanks her back, making her bounce off his chest with a similar amount of force as the time they met last week.

She stills as he catches her and holds her with both hands just above her elbows.

"That wasn't soon enough," he says.

He reaches the palm of his right hand across her jaw and moves it around to grip the back of her neck. She sucks in air as he bends his head in an attempt to place his lips on her open mouth. He moves in slowly, making sure she doesn't have any objections before they touch.

I watch the light from the streetlamp narrow until there is nothing escaping between their two bodies.

Their slow, gentle, exploratory kiss becomes more passionate as they get to know each other. Not only am I angry that she is kissing this man she hardly knows, but I'm also furious that it's escalating so quickly right in front of my eyes. I can't control it, and I need to control it.

I can hear my tendons crunch as I move my jaw back and forth. This is not what I want. This is not what I have planned for Penelope. This must stop.

I squeeze my hand into my jean pocket and pull out my car key fob. I press the tiny red panic button and hunker down as low into my seat as possible.

Constant honking, alarm bells, and flashing lights go off. I wish I could see them part from each other, but I need to stay low, so they don't see me. I let the alarm go off for a good twenty seconds before turning it off.

I wait, hunched low for another twenty, before slowly bringing my head up to take a peek, testing to see if it's safe to sit up.

They're not looking this direction, but I did my job. I broke them up enough for Penelope to go into her apartment. Alone. Her front door closes just in time for me to witness it. Nathan remains in the same spot by the mailbox, but his eyes are on Penelope's door. He doesn't turn to leave until a few beats after her door closes behind her.

I, on the other hand, stay for several hours.

TEN

I clear my throat, staring at myself in the bathroom mirror. I repeat my speech to my reflection. It doesn't look like me. I know how to dress for an occasion, but I'm not a black-tie kind of guy.

I look like a fucking penguin.

My light-brown hair tries to curl as it hangs down past my ears. I should have gotten a haircut yesterday instead of watching Penelope get ready for her date. Still, the gel keeps it in place enough to pass for someone who belongs at a function like this— someone deserving of such a prestigious award.

I straighten my wide black bow tie against my crisp white shirt. Just enough starch for it to look pressed against my chest and not give in to wrinkles with the heavy black jacket. Everything sits where it should. Except my eyes. My green eyes have shadows cast around them. My eye sockets are sunken in and dark from too many sleepless nights. Like last night.

I sat in my car, staring at Penelope's window, for four hours. The first thirty minutes were spent listening to her conversation with Brandy about her date with Nathan. I got hard, listening to her talk about how his kiss had made her feel. But, when I realized I hadn't created that experience for her, I felt angry.

The rest of the time was spent just watching her window and listening to her breathe as she slept. I could have stayed longer, but I didn't want to risk falling asleep and having another run-in with Officer Smith.

I grab my flash cards and smack them against the bathroom marble countertop. After perfectly lining up the bottom edges, I slide them in my inside breast pocket.

The banquet room is buzzing with professors, alumni, and prestigious graduate students. They're all forming groups, trying to connect with someone higher up on the scholastic chain than they are.

Everyone is dressed to the nines. The women are all wearing long gowns. Most are sparkling with sequins, but some are shiny satin. This is the Academy Awards of Tafford, and I am the guest of honor. I imagine what it would be like for Penelope to see me here.

Would she like the way I look—clean-shaven and in a tuxedo?

No, I should have gotten a fucking haircut yesterday.

But, most of all, I wonder what she would look like in a gown designed just for her body. Something that attempts to match the magic and glow that she has when she moves in a room.

"Alexander Bishop." Dean Schumaker turns around as I nearly pass him. He reaches his hand out to shake mine, forcing me to face his group of schmoozers. If I could get out of this, I would. "We were just talking about you."

"Well"—I try to smile, feigning politeness, but, really, I hate this shit—"nobody likes to be spoken about behind their back. I hope you were discussing my research and not me."

"Astounding, just astounding." A man steps forward and shakes my hand after I release Schumaker's.

"Alex," the Dean says, "this is Professor Richard Cuffton and his wife, May. Richard owns—"

"Sci Gen Labs," I cut him off. "Yes, I'm familiar with you. You're the source of many of our grants, including mine. Many Tafford students move on to work in your labs. It's a pleasure to meet you, sir."

"Please, call me Richard," he says and puts his arm around me, shielding me from his wife and the Dean for a more private conversation. "Alexander—"

"Alex," I correct him.

He nods. "Alex, I've been watching you closely over the years. I know you have many offers across the country for your post-doctoral program, but I'll stop at nothing to get you at Sci Gen. Together," he goes on with more emphasis, "we can really change the future with genetic mapping."

I move my head up and down, as if considering his offer. There have been many. And Sci Gen has made the most breakthroughs in the industry. I'm aware that they have taken partial credit for my work since the grant was funded through the company.

But thoughts of Penelope hold me back. She hasn't made her decision on where she'll continue her education after she earns her bachelor's degree. I know she's considering UCLA or Harvard, but thankfully, they are too far away from her mother. I don't think she would move more than a drive away from her. Sci Gen Labs are north of Chico, a two-hour drive from here, but even farther from Berkeley, where I suspect she'll be applying to graduate school soon.

"I'll definitely keep that in mind."

He leans in a little closer, as if to tell me a secret. "Unlimited resources," he mutters slowly so that I can soak up every part of each word.

Most budding scientists would come at the mention of unlimited resources. I understand he's talking about finances as well. There's no limit to what he would provide me.

"I'll consider your offer," I say curtly and reach out my hand again for a departing shake. "It was nice to meet you, Richard."

People are beginning to take their seats and have their glasses filled with wine, champagne, or cognac, readying themselves for the banquet to officially begin.

"I'm sure we'll speak again soon," he tells me. He reluctantly lets me go without further conversation.

Treading across the maroon carpet, I find the round table of eight where I've been designated to sit. It's near the front where the podium is. I'm placed perfectly for being the guest of honor.

Dean Schumaker finds his seat at my table along with two of our leading professors in the genetics department and their wives. They learn from me more than the other way around. The seat to my left is empty, except for the vision of Penelope by my side.

"Alex, you didn't bring a date?" Diane Schumaker asks.

I pick up my black napkin and place it on my lap. "No, ma'am. I suppose I'm too busy with my research for dating."

Satisfied with my answer, she smiles sympathetically and leans back. A group of servers approach our table, and in unison, they each place a plate of salad in front of each of us.

I turn my head to say, "Thank you," and meet familiar brown eyes.

"Michelle," I say softly with surprise.

"Alex," she whispers, equally shocked to see me. "What are you doing here?"

"Lucky to be invited," I humbly explain to her.

She smiles quickly at me. "I've got to go, but maybe I'll see you later."

Her hair is pulled back and pinned into a bun. She looks like every other server here, except I'm familiar enough with her to pick her out among the other black button-down shirts, black pants, and long black ties. They're all meant to blend in and match. But, now that I know she's here, Michelle stands out to me.

We sit through three courses before Michelle serves me my dessert. She whispers as she sets down the dish, "I made sure you got the chocolate. The vanilla is terrible."

What a sweet and thoughtful girl. What she's doing with Kevin is beyond me.

After enough clinking of silverware being set down on the ceramic plates, Dean Schumaker stands and approaches the podium.

"Good evening," he speaks into the microphone. "Thank you all for attending this evening's banquet."

Blah, blah, blah.

I would love nothing more than to be home or outside Penelope's apartment instead of sitting here, listening to Schumaker go on and on about his university. I drown out the sound and stare off, as if I were listening intently. Really though, I'm bored to tears.

"...soon be our country's leading geneticist, Alexander Bishop."

The sound of my name brings me back to reality. This is my cue. I scoot my gold-painted chair back and smooth down the front of my tuxedo, flattening any wrinkles that might have formed while eating my meal.

I give a few nods to random places in the room, acknowledging the applause. I spot Michelle leaning against the back wall with a few of her coworkers. She nods at me, impressed, and politely claps her fingers to her palm for my benefit. I give her an extra tilt of my head, accepting her praise.

Once I reach the podium and accept my small plaque for an award from Schumaker's hands, it takes a few moments for the eruption of cheers and clapping to calm down. Everyone stood as I made my way to the stage, but they are now beginning to take their seats. All eyes are on me.

I pull out my three index cards and clear my throat. "I'd like to see a show of hands. How many here believe they know who they are?"

A sea of arms goes up. I assume everyone in the room raised their hand.

"I see. You all know who you are and how you feel," I confirm with the room.

People nod and agree, waiting for me to make my point.

"What if I said you were wrong? That who you think you are is only a perception of yourself and the reality you've created in your imagination? You probably believe that your feelings on a matter could change. You can grow and thrive and flower with new experiences. But, no. Science is more exact than that. What if I told you"—I point to a stranger, a random person sitting in the middle of the room—"that I can know you better than you know yourself?" I shift my cards to the next one.

"Our genetic DNA is concrete, and it doesn't have feelings or emotions. We are made up of predetermined building blocks that design every aspect of ourselves, including our perceived feelings. And I have found not only a way to study it and analyze it, but to also build it."

Some of the attendees seem uncomfortable with my remarks about the future of genetics, but Richard Cuffton looks, as if he were creaming his pants from listening to me speak.

"It's been a beautiful journey for me here at Tafford," I go on. "I have so many to thank for my success and continued research." I thank many of the staff members, Dean Schumaker, the university itself, and—most eager of them all—Richard Cuffton of Sci Gen for their generous donations and grant support.

The end of my speech is welcomed with a standing ovation and applause. I bow my head, accepting their accolades. I hold up my award for them to all appreciate one last time before I exit the stage.

I greet several people before I sit down again. Perhaps the entire room. Most of the party guests are grouping again and continuing their conversations and budding relationships, as they were before we sat down for dinner. I would like to rest for a moment, allowing a few minutes to pass before making my exit. I can't leave too soon, or there will be too many follow-up e-mails and phone calls. I need to let people know that I am here and among them.

"Can I take your picture for the school paper?" I hear a voice from behind me.

As I turn around, I'm faced with a camera, ready to fire.

Defensively, I take my hand and cover my face with it. "No, no." I don't take my hand away until the camera is lowered to the woman's hip.

"Dean Schumaker wanted us to cover the banquet. We need a photo," she whines.

My face contorts in annoyance. "Here," I say, holding up my plaque before setting it back down on the white table linen, "take a picture of this."

"But—" she begins to protest.

"Under no circumstances," I scold her, "do I ever want my picture in the paper. Do you understand me?"

She places her hand on her hip and snaps a quick picture of the award sitting on the table. "Thanks," she says sarcastically before walking away, pouting.

"*Jeeez*," Michelle draws out. "Camera shy?" She's sitting at the empty place setting to my left.

"I just don't care for the attention," I explain. I don't care for her question either. Although I do welcome her company right now.

"Congratulations," she says with so much sincerity. "I knew you were bright, but I didn't realize how much you'd accomplished here."

I give a polite smile. "Well, we study in different departments."

Michelle is a Psychology graduate student, like Penelope. But I'm sure they don't know each other since Penelope only takes undergraduate classes right now. Plus, I would know if they knew each other.

"What is Kevin up to this evening?" I ask, trying to be polite and make small talk.

Michelle thinks about my question for a moment. She might be going through the process of elimination, like I am. Kevin knew I would be here, so he wouldn't have asked me to join him at the club. However, that wouldn't have stopped him from going alone.

She shrugs. "At home, I suppose."

I consider putting her out of her misery and filling her in on what a secretly horrible person her boyfriend is. She can do so much better. But I still need her, especially now that Nathan is in the picture. I'm going to dedicate my week to finding something that will get rid of him. Maybe then, I'll expose Kevin to Michelle.

ELEVEN

Nathan Barker grew up in Sacramento. He was a popular track and field athlete in high school but didn't have a serious relationship until his freshman year of college. They dated a little over a year and broke up a few months before he traveled abroad.

He was telling the truth about his boring upbringing. His parents haven't even had a hiccup in their practice. Hard to do these days when everyone is eager to sue for a piece of the pie.

Growing up, my father was constantly in court, battling the latest attack.

"It's part of the business," he would say.

But, as I grew older, I learned it was just part of him. I'm not ungrateful for my trust, but I plan to stay far away from my father. Not that he has ever wanted it any other way.

Nathan isn't here on a scholarship, so I can't get that taken away from him. I could ask to have him expelled from the university, but then I would have to explain myself. His parents are paying his tuition. They're likely comfortable doing so, but he didn't have the affluent upbringing that I did.

That leads me to where I am now, sitting in a waiting room, hoping to find something interesting from being closer to Nathan Barker's life and the ones he cares about.

"Mr. Bishop?"

I look up to the receptionist behind the Plexiglas partition.

"Dr. Barker will see you now. A nurse will meet you on the other side of that door." She points to the solid door to the left.

I collect my briefcase and follow the slightly overweight nurse toward exam room B. On our way there, I try to absorb my surroundings and get a bearing on the practice's layout. There's a closed door across from the receptionist's desk without a letter associating it with an exam room.

"Here we are." She gestures inside a room in the middle of the long hallway.

Wrapping blue fabric around my upper arm, she takes my blood pressure—*normal*—and other vitals. Then, she proceeds to ask me simple questions about my health and daily activities. I don't smoke, I don't practice unprotected sex, and I don't drink to excess. I exercise as often as Penelope does, and that seems to be three times a week at the student rec center—as long as nothing comes up with her studies.

"What are you here to see the doctor about?" the nurse asks.

"Just a general consultation. I'm looking to switch practitioners."

I move around, adjusting my position, and create a series of crackling noises from the paper beneath me. The fluorescent lighting in here won't do well for the bags under my eyes. And I still need that damn haircut.

"Dr. Barker will be right in," the nurse informs me before leaving the room.

It was a five-minute drive from campus, and luckily, they had an opening with Nathan's mom during Penelope's Psychology 404 class. If this can go quickly enough, I'll be back to campus in time for Penelope to leave class and study in the library for an hour. I'd like to leave articles on the dangers of motorcycles and their fatality rates near table eight.

A light knock on the door lets me know the good doctor is here. I'm hoping to find something horribly unethical or unattractive, something that would turn Penelope off from entering any further into a relationship with Nathan and his family ties.

What I find is a visually pleasant midlife woman. Her black hair is down but brushed nicely, leaving it in controlled waves.

"Hello"—she glances down at her folder—"Alexander." Her hand reaches out to shake mine.

She's a little shorter than I am, but that puts us at eye-level as I remain seated on the exam bed.

"Nice to meet you, Dr. Barker." I reach out and test the delicateness of her small hand.

Immediately after letting go, she turns to wash her hands in the nearby sink. "So, you're just looking for a new physician?" she asks, still scrubbing while the water runs over her hands.

"Yes. I'm considering taking up a more permanent residence here and thought I should secure a doctor before I need regular physicals."

She smiles at me. "I don't see anything wrong with that," she says, drying her hands with a paper towel. Dr. Barker takes a seat on the round swivel stool in the corner. Scooting it closer, she asks, "Are you on any prescription medications?"

I've already answered these questions. "No."

She keeps her eyes down on my file to read a few lines. "So, you've been treated at the Tafford student clinic in the past?" Her hands go to the top of the file, and she raises her head with a tight purse in her lips, trying to conceal a smile. "I guess that means you're a student there."

"Yes, ma'am."

Now, she unleashes her smile. "My son is an International Studies major. He was abroad last year, but he starts classes again in a few weeks."

I know.

"That's nice." I tried to sound interested, but I'm afraid my bitterness came through.

"Okay," she says and then looks back down to my file. "Alexander, the only thing that concerns me is your lack of sleep. It's perfectly understandable for you to be up late studying, but if there's any way for you to get in at least seven hours of sleep a night, your body will really thank you for it."

I nod. "Yes, it's just that the workload is so heavy at this stage in school," I lie.

I could conduct my research in my sleep if I needed to. It's Penelope that keeps me up at night.

She reaches her hand over and places it on my knee. "I know, sweetheart, but it'll all be worth it once you get your degree. Hang in there a little longer."

Her jovial face and warm smile travel through her hand and melt into my knee on contact. It's her instincts as a mother that made her touch me, wanting to soothe my faux worries.

I'm ashamed by how much I like her and am enjoying her company in exam room B. Penelope would like her, too.

"Alexander, do you have any questions for me?" Dr. Barker asks, taking her hand from my knee and standing with my file tucked under her arm.

Yes, what's the worst thing your son has ever done? "No, ma'am."

She reaches for the door handle but remains facing me. I watch, transfixed, as a lone hair falls from around her shoulders. It teeters like a feather falling to the floor.

"Well then," she says, grabbing my attention again, "you just let us know if anything comes up. Take your time. You can leave when you're ready."

I nod in her direction and let her exit the room. Once the door closes, my eyes move directly to the floor. I bend down and pick up the fallen hair. My breathing slows as I narrow my eyes to take as close a look as I can with the naked eye.

The gray is trying to pop out, but the hair dye has masked it once it gets a few centimeters from the root.

"I wish you could tell me something," I say to this intrinsic part of her being. I consider bagging it, but I quickly remind myself that she is not my subject. I open my fingers and let it fall back down to the floor.

I take what I came with—my briefcase and jacket—and then I exit the exam room. In my peripheral, I spot Dr. Barker down the hall, near the door to the waiting room.

She's handing the manilla folder that holds my medical information to the receptionist. "You can file this now," she tells her.

Immediately, the receptionist takes the folder and walks to the other side of the hall, reappearing a few moments later.

Slowly, I begin walking down the hallway toward the exit and the file room. I look to the left and see the receptionist is handing paperwork to another patient while talking to her about insurance.

Instead of walking straight to leave, I quickly turn right and am out of sight before the receptionist can look my way.

It's dark, and I don't dare turn on the lights. I'll need to move fast. Both walls are lined with horizontal white filing cabinets, four stacked on top of each other. My hand reaches for the middle drawer in the first row of the system. I pull it out slowly, as not to create any noise from the metal track.

Perfect...letter B.

I run my fingers over the tabs quickly, scanning for the familiar Barker name. I wouldn't be surprised if I didn't find anything. Just wishful thinking. Although his parents wouldn't necessarily treat their kids, I'm sure they have their medical records on hand.

I find four files with the last name Barker. I'm about to pull out the one labeled Nathan, but I pause for a moment. Something else strikes me as important. The emblem for the Sacramento County Sheriff's Department is peeking out of the corner of Carol Barker's file.

This must be his sister. Interesting.

The soft padding of tennis shoes rubs against the carpet a few feet outside the door. The intensity builds, and I know someone is getting close. I grab Carol's file and slide it into my briefcase. Two steps are all it takes for me to be in the doorframe, and one step from being in the clear, I'm struck by the body of the slightly overweight nurse.

After she regains balance from the impact, she looks at me with surprise and crinkles her brows in suspicious confusion. "What were you doing in there?"

"I'm so sorry. You startled me." I place my hands on her shoulders and try to convince her that I mean no harm. "I'm just looking for the restroom. Can you point me in the right direction?"

"Yes," she agrees, still looking at me suspiciously. She points down the hall in the opposite direction of the waiting room. "Past the receptionist stand, second door on the right."

"Got it." I head in that direction, moving fast, so the moment can quickly leave her mind.

She'll soon chalk it up to nothing but a misunderstanding and forget we ran into each other.

I use my excuse to relieve myself, but then I exit the building as soon as possible. I'll feel a lot better once I get my briefcase and the documents I took into my car and out of this facility.

As I leave, I pass three other patients in the waiting room. A sign of a healthy business. Not too overcrowded, so it seems they manage their patients well and don't overbook. I am just itching to find some dirt on these people, and reading what's in Carol's file will soon be a joy.

The early winter sunshine signals freedom once I've fully exited the office and find myself in the middle of a California strip mall. The outdoor shopping is broken up into two zoning categories—retail and commercial. There are two stories—businesses on the second floor and shops with a ground-floor entrance. The metal stairs creak as I descend to the parking lot.

I reach for my door handle, attempting to unlock my vehicle with the touch sensor. I don't even get so far as to hear the short beep and click of the unlocking when I'm struck with an all-too familiar sound.

"Alex, what the fuck are you doing here?"

TWELVE

"Kevin." I try to sound pleasantly surprised, but I'm not. I didn't expect to bump into him here, but I also know he has a knack for showing up at inopportune times—like this one.

Michelle is trailing behind him. She skips to catch up.

"Hi, Alex. What are you doing here?" she asks once she nears.

How am I going to get out of this one? The last thing I want is anyone from campus knowing that I've been in to see Dr. Barker.

Kevin takes his hand out of his pocket and puts his arm around the back of Michelle's shoulders. "I was just asking him that."

I look up at the business signs and find the perfect excuse. "I'm here for a haircut," I simply say and turn to open my car door. "I just mindlessly brought my briefcase and realized I didn't need it." I drop my bag on the driver's seat and close the door.

"Ha," Kevin scoffs. "Mindless. Doesn't sound like you. Are you sure you're all right?" He laughs and slaps my back.

I ignore his attempt at making fun of me. "Better question is, what are the two of you doing here?" I look directly at Kevin since I have no clue about Michelle's daily schedule. "Aren't you supposed to be leading a discussion group right now?"

This gives me the opportunity to glance down at my watch. Penelope's class gets out in twenty minutes. If I get a haircut, I'll surely miss her. But I can always catch up with her in the library. She doesn't need to study much for her nutrition class, so she's probably going to get ahead on her psychology syllabus.

"We just went out for breakfast," Michelle answers my first question for him. She turns to the side to fit snugly under Kevin's arm. Her hand goes up to rest on his chest.

This disturbs me, and I can't understand why I care about her love life. She's so plain. But, with that known, she's still a very pleasant girl, and I wish she weren't being victimized by Kevin and his philandering. She's unknowing and innocent. But she should know better since she's a psychology graduate student. She should have picked up on the signs of his flawed character. I spotted them within thirty seconds of meeting Kevin years ago.

Why can't she see it?

"Yeah," Kevin pipes in. "I moved to the afternoon discussion group. Professor Carrington likes to switch it up after midterms. My Wednesday mornings are free."

I'd rather stop wasting time talking to Kevin and get that haircut now. I don't want to miss Penelope in the library.

"It was good bumping into you two."

I nod at Kevin, but when my eyes meet Michelle's, I return the smile she's offering me. She has average brown eyes, nothing special about them, but they warm me with her smile.

"I hope you have a good day," I say specifically to her.

"You, too," she returns.

I walk past them, toward the barbershop at the end of the two-story strip mall.

Kevin turns as I pass him. "Club tonight?" he asks with his arm still around Michelle. He turns to look at her. "Sorry, honey, I know you've got to work."

I want to roll my eyes, but I remain composed. "I'll think about it."

I don't know what Penelope's plans are yet. There's usually a band playing on Wednesday nights. It's not uncommon for her to go out, especially once she gets ahead on her studies.

I brush a fallen clipped hair off my shoulder. They're probably everywhere. Those black capes never seem to do a great job at deterring little hairs from sticking on your clothes.

Nothing has changed since midterms two weeks ago. Only three more weeks left in the semester, and the library is just as half-empty as it typically is this time of day. The week before and during finals, it's packed with students trying to cram last-minute information.

As I near the study hall on the way to my office, I long for the smell of vanilla and violets. I hope a gust of air miraculously pushes her scent in my direction.

My hopes come crashing in on me when I notice she's not where she's supposed to be. Penelope is a creature of habit, and she should be sitting right there at table eight. I almost stop in my tracks at the realization that she's gone, but I only slow down as I pass the study hall—not slow enough for anyone to notice my reaction.

"Fuck," I say out loud once my office door is closed. *Where the hell is she?*

I look up at the clock. My haircut didn't take more than twenty minutes. She still has forty minutes before her nutrition class begins.

I'm itching to see what's in Carol Barker's file. I could stay here and go through the documents, only making sure Penelope is where she should be when her class starts. *No, the file can wait.* I need to know where she is right now.

Sitting down at my desk, I swing open the top of my silver laptop and begin tracking her phone. A few pings, and a little black dot starts bouncing up and down.

She's in the library. I zoom in as the app allows. It looks as if she might be in the back of the study hall.

I need to see her.

Leaving my office, I grab an index card, keeping my head down, and study it, as if I were trying to memorize the Dewey Decimal number of a book. I make my way toward the end of the study hall section.

After the ten rows of study tables, the room opens into a less formal area. There are sofas and large lounge chairs for students to casually read and a large gothic-looking fireplace. I stay in the back, against the wall.

Her hair illuminates the room and grabs my attention. She's sitting on a green tufted leather sofa with her back to me. Something draws me near her. It's not enough to just see her; I want to know why she's on the couch instead of at the table, like she usually is at this time of day.

I take a few steps out from the back corner and conveniently find myself parallel with a magazine stand. I step to the side of it and crouch down, pretending to sift through my options on the stand.

She's not alone. I see *his* shoe bouncing up and down as he wags his leg draped over the opposite knee. Nathan is lying down with his head on Penelope's lap, reading a book. Penelope has her own head in a book, but hers is a textbook from her psychology class. They look comfortable. They look too comfortable with each other, and it's making me very uncomfortable.

I grab the magazine closest to my hand and take it to one of the lounge chairs. I sit back in the soft high-back seat and keep the magazine open in front of my face. *National Geographic* is what I grabbed. I'm relieved it's not *Teen Vogue*. I can't focus on what's in front of me anyway, as my eyes are skimming past the pages and narrowing in on my girl.

Twenty-five minutes later, Nathan finally sits up.

"Is it time to go?" she asks after his movements prompt her to look outside of the book she's been studying. She was as engrossed in the textbook as I am with her.

Nathan leans forward on the couch to pull his phone from his back pocket. Flipping it over to see the screen and turn it on, he reads the time. "Your class is in Thompson Hall, right?"

She nods, silently answering his question.

"Yeah, we should get going. I'll walk you."

He stands and offers her his hand. She doesn't take it right away. He patiently waits while she slides her textbook inside her satchel. But then she places her delicate little hand in his and lets him help her up to her feet. Their hands don't part once they start walking.

I follow them, leaving my things in my office space.

"Want to go to the club tonight?" Penelope asks once they reach the outdoors.

The sunshine still beams, even though the weather is cooling to a California winter of mid-fifties and sixties for the next couple of months.

"Brandy really wants to see the band that's playing. You should come with us."

Nathan lifts his hand, pulling the back of hers up to his mouth. "You're the boss," he tells her. "I'm in."

That means, I'm in, too. I take my phone in my hand and text Kevin.

Alex: Club sounds good tonight. Let's meet at nine.

It doesn't take long for me to get a reply.

Kevin: Sounds good. I'm ready to party.

I know what that means. The only time he likes to *party* is when Michelle isn't around, and it usually entails other women.

They reach Thompson Hall. I lean against the side of a tree, blocking most of my body from their potential view. I can still see them, and I can't think of a reason they would need to look my way.

Nathan finally lets go of her hand. They say good-bye to each other, and she's about to walk away from him when he says, "Wait," and takes her hand again.

They stand there, staring into each other's eyes for a few seconds. She waits patiently before Nathan puts his lips together and slowly kisses her. Her lips remain closed but pressed against his so tight, there's no remaining pink surface area to be seen.

They both breathe in deeply before letting go, equally savoring the scent or the moment together.

"Good-bye, beautiful," he says softly.

She smiles a wide grin but tucks the corner of her bottom lip between her teeth. "It's only an hour. I'll see you after class."

His eyebrows move up and down, and he tucks a fallen hair behind her ear. "Might only be for an hour, but it's still a damn good excuse to kiss you."

I roll my back further around the tree, taking a moment to let out some frustration. *I'm the one who walks her to class. I'm the one who waits for her after.* I've never felt her so out of my control. My hand runs through my hair, wanting something to grip, but it slips right through. This frustrates me even more, so I slap myself—just once, hard. I need to feel the sting.

A few deep breaths later, I go back to watching them. I roll myself around the tree until they're in view again.

She starts walking backward, not wanting to look away from him. That wide grin on her face hasn't changed. "I'll see you soon."

Nathan watches her. He doesn't move until she goes into her classroom.

I'm shooting daggers at him, hoping my mood and stare might have some sort of negative physical effect on him. I want to make him suffer in some way. This isn't what I had planned for her. I was supposed to be the one bumping into her that day, but I hadn't made her ready for me yet.

Penelope disappears completely out of view. Nathan could have turned in any direction, but something made him turn toward me. My reflexes aren't fast enough to remove the scowl I know I have on my face.

He meets my stare. I try to relax but not too fast. A drastic change in expression could make him even more privy to my lurking. He looks around to see if I might possibly be looking at someone else. Luckily, there are people walking past him to head into Thompson Hall.

"Rebecca, why are you ignoring me?" I yell loudly enough for two women to turn and look at me. I start moving toward them.

Nathan understands my stare wasn't meant for him, so he walks in the other direction.

"Rebecca!" I yell one more time to seal the deal.

The girls look at each other and then look at me, confused. They stop because it's clear to them that I'm trying to approach them.

"Oh, I'm sorry," I say to them once I'm sure Nathan is out of earshot. "I thought you were someone else."

THIRTEEN

My research is nearly complete, but I still have work to do. I'm creating DNA, and I'm making it exactly what I want. I could just clone Penelope, but where's the challenge in that? Where's the progress? I need to create the code from scratch, not just copy it. But it will be just like Penelope, perfection at every curve and particle that maps her soul.

Professor Whitaker is expecting an update on my research by the end of the semester. Since Nathan entered the picture, I've spent more time than I planned following Penelope's movements. I can't give up going to the club tonight, so I'll have to spend more time during the weekdays composing something that will satisfy Whitaker. It won't take much. Two and a half weeks will be plenty of time to accomplish what I want.

I turn off the engine and expect to meet Kevin any minute. He's never late to start drinking. Penelope, Nathan, and Brandy shouldn't be far behind. They were ready to leave by the time I left her apartment.

Once I'm out of my car, I can see my reflection in the side mirror. There's a button I missed toward the bottom of my navy-blue casual dress shirt. My fingers move down and pinch the small round button through the eyelet as I look for other discrepancies. I also spot a stain on the left upper thigh of my blue jeans. I lick my thumb and rub the small spot. Between Penelope and the extra lab hours I've been trying to squeeze in, I've been pressed for time and neglecting a few chores, like laundry.

I'm getting sloppy in more ways than one. I bend down to examine my face. Acceptable, but the side of my hair could use a little work. I lick my palm and rub it against my head, matting down any stray hairs that might think about going rogue.

It's showtime. I try to pump myself up for this evening.

The club could use a little extra air-conditioning. It's still early in the evening, as far as college students would be concerned, and there's an immediate pressure of humidity once I enter the building.

As soon as the door closes behind me, I spot Kevin at the left bar. He's leaning over the countertop and whispering something in the female bartender's ear. She pushes back and pretends to be shocked by what he said, but at the same time, she makes it clear she likes whatever idea he put in her head. She purses her lips and pulls out a bottle of tequila. She looks around to make sure management isn't watching and pours two shots. Quickly, they slam the drinks back and pound the shot glasses back on the bar top. She swipes them and puts them aside, getting rid of the evidence.

Tsk, tsk, tsk... drinking on the job.

"I didn't see your car," I say to Kevin as I approach the barstool on his right so that I can face the front doors, on the lookout for Penelope and her entourage.

He turns in my direction with a shit-eating grin on his face. I can see his skin flushing as the burn of the shot courses throughout his insides. "I took a cab. I'm feeling epic tonight," he says, raising his eyebrows at the bartender.

Light from the parking lot filters in the front of the club. I scan my eyes over. *Not her.*

I debate on the level of intoxication I should achieve tonight. Kevin needs a drinking buddy until I leave. Then, this bartender—his obvious victim this evening—can take over. I also need to maintain my cover as an average college graduate student, a face in the crowd. It was reckless of me to let Nathan notice me this afternoon.

Unlike Kevin, getting drunk is not my forte. More than anything, I need to remain in control. I'll just order one drink for now, sip it slowly, and play it by ear as the night moves along.

"Whiskey and Coke," I call out to the bartender. "Well is fine," I add.

"Attaboy." Kevin slaps me on my back.

Sometimes, I wonder if he needs me as much as I need him.

PLANNING PENELOPE

Students trickle in constantly, but there's no sign of her yet. I hope they haven't changed their minds and decided on something else for the night. I pull out my cell phone, attempting to track her location, when I know. I can feel the energy in the room change. I know she's here before I even look toward the doors. But I still need to see her.

After it's placed in front of me, I raise my glass and listen to the ice cubes clink together as a slow stream enters my mouth. My eyes peer over the rim of my highball.

Penelope and Brandy glide inside the club, as if there were an angelic glow around them. My heart beats to the pounding thud of the drummer warming up onstage.

My rhythm slows when I spot their third wheel trailing close behind my strawberry vision. He's so close on her back, and all I can think about is his erection likely probing her backside.

I grab my drink tighter and tilt the glass back further, giving my throat the burn it suddenly aches for.

"Looks as if you're feeling epic tonight, too," Kevin says, admiring my commitment.

Not exactly.

"It's just been a long day, but I've got to slow down. A lot of lab time tomorrow," I explain.

That'll be good. That sets me up to stay in the club and keep an eye on Penelope but panders to Kevin's expectations at the same time.

He's trying to start a conversation with me, but his eyes keep moving to the bartender. The lights are so dim in here, I wonder if he notices the blemish on the corner of her mouth, masked by layers of makeup.

"Why"—I wait for his attention to be back on me—"would you be with Michelle when you're clearly interested in other women?" My question comes from a sincere place. I not only despise disloyalty, but I also truly don't understand it.

He shrugs. "You can't just be with one woman." He says it like it's something I should understand. "Michelle is the kind of woman you take home to meet your mom." He takes a sip of his poorly mixed margarita. At least he's sticking to one type of liquor. "Eventually," he adds.

The room fills with more music as the band's warm-up seems to come to an end. It's almost time for their set to begin and the

79

club to become packed with young adults escaping the stresses of higher education.

Penelope, Brandy, and Nathan sit at a high-top, center stage. Nathan stands and says something to the women before turning and heading in this direction.

I raise my glass and toss the rest of my drink down my throat. I need an excuse to switch sides with Kevin, so my back will be to Nathan when he reaches the bar.

"So, eventually, you'll be with one woman? You just don't want to be monogamous now?" I ask as I move behind him to the other side. I raise my hand, signaling Kevin's victim of the night so that she knows I'm ready for another drink.

I'm twisted, so I'm fully facing Kevin. Nathan is at my back and waiting patiently for the bartender's attention. The room fills up quickly, and everyone wants a drink once they arrive, so every now and then, I feel pressure from Nathan's shoulder or arm. *I wish I could reach back and break his arm.*

"Maybe," Kevin says. "I can't imagine ever being with one woman for the rest of my life."

I hear Nathan scoff, possibly overhearing our conversation. Part of me wants to like the idea that he abhors cheaters like Kevin, but the other part of me despises him for everything that he is, including an eavesdropper.

My drink arrives, and I grab it as soon as it hits the bar top.

"You wouldn't understand," Kevin adds, drinking more of his margarita. He'll need another one any second. I'm sure his whore will rush to his order. "You don't have a girlfriend."

My hand grips tighter around my drink. The sweat perspiring on the outside of the glass, caused from the cold liquid inside, moves around my fingers when they squeeze tighter. I fight the urge to slam the glass over Kevin's head. I fight even harder not to scream at him in defense. What I have with Penelope is so much more than a girlfriend. The love, care, and time I put into her is so much more special than any superficial relationship he has ever been remotely close to having. Instead, I just nod, pretending to agree with his asinine statement.

I'm relieved when Nathan is gone. I don't like him anywhere near me or Penelope.

The crowded bar erupts with screams, cheers, and applause as the band enters the stage for the first show out of two planned for the night. The lead singer laughs at one of the excited bar patrons and points into the crowd. Every member of the band is young enough, and they seem to be recognized by enough people for me to assume they're students at the university.

"Anyway," Kevin shouts now that the band has started and the noise becomes a constant buzz, "I've been thinking about getting more serious with Michelle. Maybe I'll ask her if she wants to come home with me for Christmas."

I look away from him, so I can roll my eyes. "You just turned her down for meeting her parents over Thanksgiving, and now, you want her to meet yours?" *What a fucking idiot.*

"I don't really care about her parents. I'll meet them eventually. It's my mom's approval I need."

He must have mommy issues.

"I've been thinking, maybe I'll propose after we've been together a year—after graduation, after we have jobs." He considers something and nods, agreeing with himself. "Yeah, that'll be good timing."

You've gotta be shitting me.

He has reached an all-time low as a presumptuous prick.

I look over at Penelope's table and read their lips.

"I know the bass player. He's in my economics class," Brandy says to the table. "So hot." She fans herself and laughs with Penelope.

Nathan smiles at the women, amused.

Brandy moves away from her chair. "Come on, let's go dance."

Penelope's eyes immediately move to Nathan's, waiting, wanting to know what his reaction will be to the idea of dancing.

His chin moves up. "Yeah, let's go."

Penelope smiles, and Nathan takes her hand, following a bouncing Brandy onto the dance floor.

"Another round," I murmur loudly for the bartender to hear.

Kevin winks at her, agreeing with my order.

"It's your life," I say to Kevin, going back to his conversation about his relationship with Michelle.

Unfortunately, it's her life, too. But, right now, his relationship with her is working in my favor, so it is not the time for me to lose momentum on my closeness with Penelope.

I grab my drink as soon as it's set down and gesture my head away from the bar. "Come on, let's go hang somewhere else." I want to move to the table Penelope was at before it's taken by someone else.

"But I like the view here," Kevin says, staring at a mischievously grinning bartender.

I lean down closer to his ear, so I don't have to yell so loudly. "You know where to find her. She's not going anywhere. Come on."

Kevin agrees by picking up his drink and following me to the table Penelope once occupied.

I reach out as soon as I'm at arm's length and set down my cocktail. "Sorry," I say to a couple of women who were about to take the spot. I take the far-left chair, the one Penelope was sitting on.

I notice a glowing strand of hair on the seat and try not to stare too long. Reaching down to pick it up before I move to sit, I relish the feel of it between my fingers. I wonder what it would be like to run the strand across my tongue. *Would it taste as good as she smells?*

Slyly, without anyone noticing, I push the lone strand of hair into my front pocket.

The sunken dance floor is close to where we are. With so many bodies shoved together and moving around so much, it might be hard to spot one person, but I can't take my eyes off her. Kevin must think I'm interested in the band, but I have only one interest here.

They dance for nearly forty minutes, during which time Nathan leaves the floor twice to get the girls more drinks, taking care of Brandy just as he's trying to tend to Penelope. Her order is the same as always—vodka tonic on the rocks. Nathan guards her, matching her beats but protecting her from other students bumping into her while she takes sips.

Her eyes barely leave his, and his never leave hers. Mine never leave *her*.

Kevin leans on his elbows. "Look at all those chicks."

Lucky for him, he's not looking at Penelope. I haven't thought much about how I would react to him eyeing my girl, but right now, I'm almost hoping for someone to kill. If Kevin so much as shows interest, so be it.

"Maybe we should get down there. I want to grind on that one." He looks pointedly at a specific woman on the dance floor.

I think about that. I have enough liquid courage in me to feel fearless. I could go down there and be another body on the floor, bumping and brushing against Penelope without anyone thinking twice about it. But I fucked up today. It's too soon for me to risk Nathan seeing my face again.

"What about your bartender?" I remind him.

He smirks. "Like you said, I know where to find her. Speaking of, I can go for another round. You?"

I shake my head. Knowing I've probably had more than I intended, I need to slow down. Kevin, on the other hand, speeds up.

When the next band comes on, Brandy finds her way to the bass player she was fanning herself over.

You're supposed to be with Penelope, not chasing starving artists. I want to scold her for leaving Penelope alone to be touched by Nathan.

But they're not alone. I'm watching along with a bar full of other people.

As far as they're concerned, it's just the two of them now. With Brandy's absence, their stares into each other's eyes become more intense, and their movements slow. I want to dive down and cut through whatever is going on between them.

He runs his hands from her wrists, up her arms, and over her shoulders. I can almost feel her shudder at his touch. His left hand lowers and moves past her side to her back. His right hand moves higher to cup her cheek. She lets the weight of her head fall onto his palm, exposing her stretched neck. I can feel the pulsation coming from its vein.

My stomach tightens, my jaw clenches, and every muscle in my body tenses.

"Shots," Kevin announces, slamming down two shots of tequila. "On the house," he adds.

His timing couldn't have been better. Penelope and Nathan consume each other's mouths with no fear of onlookers.

I take the shot and slam the glass back down, creating a loud smack on the wooden surface. I feel no burn; that sensation is long gone. Wiping my mouth with the back of my hand, I move to dive down and rescue Penelope from this imminent mistake she might be thinking about making with him tonight.

Kevin's hand swings over and stops my chest from moving forward. "Hey, what's wrong?" he asks. "What's with that look on your face? I've never seen you take a shot like that. It's as if you were angry with the tequila."

I try to shake this mood looming over me. My attention goes back to my so-called friend. "Nothing. I've just got my mind on my research." *Penelope.*

"You just need to get laid more often." He laughs at me, struggling to have a good time.

He's right. I haven't had sex in a month. I've been so distracted. I'll take care of that tomorrow night. I pull out my phone and set a reminder.

I look over to see Nathan whispering something in Penelope's ear. She nods her head and agrees. Taking each other's hand, they walk around the outside of the dance floor and find Brandy.

Good, they're leaving.

Penelope's back is to me, so I can't read her lips.

Brandy leans up and shakes her head. "I'm gonna stay here," she says and moves her eyes toward the bass player.

Nathan leans in to say something to Brandy.

Brandy smiles sweetly, saying, "Okay."

Faster than I can wrap my head around it, they're at the entrance and leaving the building.

Oh no, she is not fucking him tonight. Not on my watch.

FOURTEEN

"Kevin, I just realized I booked extra lab hours, and it starts really early. I'm going to call it a night." I lean over and place my hand on his shoulder, gripping it as guylike as I can. "You can thank the bartender for me." I lean back, grab the empty shot glass, and hold it up.

Kevin's sly grin spreads across his face. I don't have to look at his pants to know he's hard at just the thought of spending the rest of the night with the bartender. He might not even make it out of here before fucking her in a dirty bathroom. More power to him, but I've got somewhere else to be.

"Will do," he says as I leave the table.

I know they have a head start, but I'm not far behind. I rush as soon as I near the creaking metal doorframes, trying to figure out a way to stop Penelope from sleeping with him tonight.

I saw the way they were looking at each other, and it makes me panic. My eyes squint when the door opens, and my pupils try to adjust to the streetlights surrounding the parking lot.

"Alex," a voice says.

I see a blur in front of me. It slowly comes into focus and reveals Michelle's face. The angelic way the lights dance around her changes my mood. For a quick moment, I forget about Penelope and why I'm in such a hurry.

Still holding the door open, I say, "I thought you had to work tonight?"

"I did. I just got off a little early, so I thought I would meet up with you guys." She changed her clothes, and she looks like she belongs here with the other partying students, but her hair is still pulled back into a bun, like it was during the banquet. "Is Kevin still here?" she asks.

If I let her in, I'll be exposing Kevin's cheating. I can't let her find out about his behavior. They'll stop seeing each other, and I won't have the benefit of having a wingman. Kevin wants what he can't have. If they break up, it will eat at Kevin until he has her back. I fear this will change things too drastically. I need to keep things the way they are.

On the other hand, Kevin is the scum of the earth and everything I hate about human nature. I would be saving Michelle from a potential lifetime of misery. Plus, if I get rid of her, I can still follow Penelope and come up with a plan to make sure she doesn't sleep with Nathan. I can pull the fire alarm in their building, if I can't think of anything better.

But then again, there's a twinge at the bottom of my stomach that doesn't want to hurt Michelle. Kevin will inevitably hurt her. I have no problems using either of them for my benefit to advance my connection with Penelope, but do *I* want to be the reason Michelle is in pain?

He can dig his own grave. Michelle is a smart girl, and she'll figure it out eventually. Hopefully before things get too far. Until I get rid of Nathan, I can't let their relationship change anything. I'll get to Penelope as soon as I'm able.

"I'm not sure," I tell her.

She looks at me, unsure about what I've said. She's right; I came here to meet with him, so how can I not know whether he's inside?

I put my hand on her shoulder and apply more pressure than necessary, swaying side to side.

"Alex, are you okay?" she asks, placing her hand on top of mine, gaining leverage for herself as I shift my weight and sway side to side.

"I was shust about to drife home," I slur.

She moves her head closer to mine, studying my face. I purposely avoid eye contact.

"Alex, you're drunk."

She's not completely wrong. But am I as completely incoherent as I'm pretending to be? No.

I make sure to let my weight go and allow my body to move freely in the air, as if I didn't have equilibrium. I take my hand off her shoulder and reach into my pocket. I pull out my key fob. "I'm just gonna go home. See you later, Michelle."

Her eyes widen, and she reacts in panic. "You can't drive. You need to take a cab or call student DD."

"No," I spit quickly. "I would never leave my car in a parking lot. I have to get my car home. It's not far," I falsely reassure her.

She steps in front of me and grasps on to each of my shoulders, the widest part of my body. "Look, you can't drive. I'll drive your car home."

Yes. A feeling of satisfaction floods back to me. It's been a few weeks since I've felt this way. Always as planned.

I press the button to make my car sing two rows down. The front lights flash off and on twice, and Michelle knows exactly where to go. I hand her the key fob as we get close.

This is the first time I've ever sat in the passenger seat of my own car. It's the same seat and only a few inches away from where I normally sit, but it feels so different.

I'm uneasy with the idea of Michelle driving but not enough to stop it. I'm making her drive me home. I'm still in control even though she's the one in the driver's seat. She puts the fob in the cup holder between us and presses the button to start the engine. I have to tell her where to turn and what streets to drive on.

I wasn't lying when I said it wasn't far. My apartment is less than a five-minute drive. Other than the directions I'm barking, the car ride is silent. Every now and then, she glances over at me, her brows creasing, and once, she looks down at the key fob between us.

What is she thinking? Is she judging me for being drunk? Is she mad that I left her boyfriend high and dry at the bar? Ha. Does she question the authenticity to how inebriated I am?

Everything is going the way I want, but not knowing what's going through her mind is bothering me.

"Over there." I point to the right side of the road. "That's my building. You can just park in front."

She pulls over with the perfect amount of space between my car tires and the curb, and she takes a deep breath as she presses her pointer finger on the engine button, turning off the car. I still, anticipating her impending words.

"Are we friends?" she asks once the engine comes to a complete quiet.

Her question surprises me. I've never thought much of it. Kevin is my friend, but he's also someone I loathe associating myself with. Michelle is someone I very much enjoy associating myself with, but I can't consider her my friend.

"You're Kevin's girlfriend," is all I can think to say before knowing exactly where she's going with this.

She laughs through her nose—not a laugh where she's truly amused, but just a whimper of a laugh, trying to find humor where she clearly isn't going to find it. "You don't think you can be friends with two people who are in a relationship with each other?"

"I've just never thought about it before." I consciously try to hold still, not giving away any physiological signs of stress. But I feel like I have an itch all over my body.

She looks down at her lap, as if she were disappointed in my response, before bringing her eyes up to mine. Her sad brown eyes don't seem so plain anymore. Until now, I've never noticed there's an ember illuminating from her pupils. The spark melts into the rest of her irises, like a caramel espresso.

I'm not sure I've ever been this close to notice.

"You're not drunk, are you?" She deadpans her stare, not giving me an inch to move or show vulnerability.

I stare back and her, just breathing, contemplating my answer. "I drank plenty at the club," I finally state.

"But you didn't need me to drive you home."

Very astute. I haven't given her enough credit. Maybe that has something to do with her choice in a lover.

I don't answer. I sit, waiting to see if she has anywhere else to go with this conversation. Right now, I want nothing more than to get out of this car.

"Why didn't you want me to go into the club?" she asks. "Is there a reason you didn't want me to see Kevin in there? Or…" Her words seem to drift off with her mind.

I'm not sure if she had an alternative question and didn't want to say it or if she's searching for one and can't find it.

As for her first actual question, she's right but not right. It has more to do with Penelope than anyone else.

Penelope. I need to get to her apartment. *Or Nathan's.*

The thought makes me clench my teeth, my jaw muscles flexing.

First, I need to get out of this conversation with Michelle. Looking back at her allows me to relax my jaw and let go of the tension. I think about answering her question carefully. "Is there a reason you're with him when you have these questions?" I wish I could reach out to her and let her know she can answer my question honestly, but I remain still.

"A reason?" she repeats. "Don't we all want to see the best in people? Isn't that what we're all looking for?"

I see the best in Penelope because she is flawless. Her DNA and who she is cannot be changed or improved. She is everything earthly and heavenly—perfection. Unlike so many others who roam in existence.

Is Michelle asking me if Kevin is cheating? I'm not sure if her peculiar questions are that specific.

I feel so out of place with her staring at me, expecting some sort of conversation. My insides move about in a way I'm not familiar with. I finally allow myself to adjust the way I'm sitting, but it doesn't change anything. I'm still uncomfortable. I see that she is asking something from me that I can't give her. I need to remove myself from this situation.

You deserve so much better, I tell her in my mind, but the words don't seem to commit to being said out loud.

I try a different tactic. This discomfort I feel provokes an anger I didn't realize I had toward her. I hastily grab the fob from the cup holder between us and get out of my car.

She meets me in the cool night breeze, standing in the driver-side doorway, still waiting for me to give her something. Confusion further covers her face. She can't understand why I've suddenly become angry. I notice three folds in her forehead as she tries to look deeper, analyzing me or scolding me with her thoughts. She pulls her neck back, as if she didn't understand something—my sudden anger perhaps—and her nostrils flare, almost like a twitch on her small nose.

Is she readying herself for my tantrum, or is she angry at the thought of me being upset with her?

"Kevin is your problem, not mine!" I yell at her, slamming my door.

I turn my back to her and enter my building. I hear a noise escape her mouth, but she doesn't actually say anything as I walk away. Once I hear the driver-side door close, I press the lock button on my fob.

I know I'm leaving her out in the cold as I enter my building, but she left me no choice. I had to remove myself from that situation. Taking the elevator up to the seventh floor, I start biting my fingernail—something I haven't done since I was a teenager.

Once I'm in my apartment, I rush to the window. I peer down and see her. She's pacing back and forth on the dark, empty sidewalk, holding her phone to her ear.

Please be calling a cab or an Uber to pick you up.

Her free arm is rubbing her other bare shoulder, trying to coax her body to get warmer. She expected to be in a sweltering club, but instead, I forced her to where she is now.

A new, discomforting feeling falls over me. My stomach turns, and my throat feels tight. I should be rushing off to whatever Penelope is doing with Nathan, but I can't get myself to leave this window. The least I can do is watch Michelle until I know she's safely in a car.

Five minutes later, she gets into the back of a black SUV.

I'm sorry. I'm not sure if I've ever sincerely wanted to say that to anyone before.

FIFTEEN

Once the SUV is out of sight, my mind and feelings return to Penelope. Only minutes after I got home, I turn and walk out the front door. I dash out of my building and start my car as soon as I'm in it.

It's possible to walk to her apartment from mine, but this is urgent. I need to get there as soon as I can, and there's no faster route than my car. Yellow lights mean nothing to me as I speed through them, daring them to defy me and turn red.

When I reach Dalton Avenue, my car and nerves begin to calm. I should have been here the whole time instead of having pointless conversations with Michelle. I turn off my lights once I reach the parking lot at the end of the street.

I'm careful as I shut my car door, not wanting to draw any attention to myself. My briefcase is still at my library office, so I'm not able to use my listening devices.

My eyes focus on her window. The lights are out, and there's no sign of movement. At least not from what I can see from the street. If they are having sex, it's not wild or exciting with thrashing limbs in every direction. I can't picture her ever making love like that anyway. She deserves something soft and sensual, passionate—not sloppy or violent.

There's not much I can do without listening in. If only I could hear her breathing. Or at least I could listen to know if two people were breathing in there.

Instead of climbing the creaking stairs up to the third floor, I move around to the back of the building. There are four main level units with their own ground entrances in the back. Nathan's apartment has to be one of them.

The night is so still, I can hear the grass crunch under my tennis shoes. I could hear anyone who might be approaching me. But then again, that means anyone would be able to hear me, too. I move to the pathway in front of the doors, closer to the building. I should have changed my clothes after the club, but Michelle got me so flustered, and I was in too much of a rush to get here to even think about changing. Right now, I'm regretting that.

The apartments seem to be a similar layout as Penelope's. These are one-bedrooms, and hers is a two, but the living room window is next to the front door, and there's another window to the side of that. I'm hoping it's a bedroom. Furthermore, I'm hoping Nathan hasn't had time to buy curtains yet.

I reach the first narrow window and stop, my body pressed against the apartment's exterior wall. There's a curtain, but the panels are just short enough for me to see through the gap between the two fabrics.

I can see the back of someone's head. *Not him.*

Definitely a man but with brown hair, not jet-black like Nathan and his mother. And not long strawberry-blonde, like Penelope.

Stepping carefully across the window, I move to the next possibility. This window has curtains, and they're completely drawn. I move my head around, searching for a gap even if it's a small one, but there's nothing to give away who's inside. I place my ear on the cold glass, listening for movement, heavy breathing, or moans. Silence.

I move to the third bedroom window.

Horizontal lines are spread across the other side of the glass. The blinds are thin and tilted just enough for me to see down into the bedroom if I have a higher vantage point. I raise myself up on the tips of my toes and peer down.

I see you.

It's him—in his queen bed with navy-blue sheets. He's asleep, turned on his right side, giving me a great view of his profile. My eyes move around the entire surface area of the bed—no Penelope. I exhale in relief.

For some reason, I don't want to leave now that I know she isn't sleeping with him. I'm feeling so territorial; even though she isn't here, I still want to rip him to shreds just for knowing he wants her. If my stare could penetrate through glass, I'd be cutting through his window like a laser.

His body and face are still. If I were in that room with him, I'd pick up the extra pillow on his bed and smother him, feeling him struggle and violently attempt to gasp until his breathing stopped.

My daydream of harming him is jolted by a shift in the air. He suddenly flinches, and his eyes spring open. I quickly roll my back against the exterior of the building and run. My tennis shoes have soft enough soles as to not make a huge clatter with my quick steps, but he still might be able to see me if he makes it to his front door in time to find me running away.

I round the corner but keep running until I make it to Dalton Avenue. I'm walking, but it's about as fast of a walk as anyone can manage. I head straight for my car and don't look back. I never heard his front door open, so I think I'm in the clear. He might not have suspected anything. He might have just had a fitful sleep and woken up naturally, thinking nothing about anything outside his window.

The campus is bright with sunlight this morning, but there's a chill whizzing through the air. Every now and then, it scoops up Penelope's hair and dances with a few light strands, twisting them into a more defined curl.

The wind has also changed the hobo guitar player's song. He stops to readjust his fingers after a few song verses. Penelope bends down and tosses her change into the red velvet-lined case as she walks by. I still haven't been back to the office to get my briefcase, so I don't have anything to contribute today. However, Penelope isn't disappointed in herself since she was able to gift him a little more than a dollar from her loose change.

Brandy is waiting at the corner for Penelope, coffee in hand. She's in a short, puffy black coat. Penelope is just in a thick-knitted sweater, so she's holding on tight to her warm cup with two hands.

I follow and prepare myself to hone in on their words as they drift back to me on this crowded street.

"Hello again," Brandy says.

The girls just left each other to get their coffees from their own preferred vendors.

Penelope smiles at her friend but keeps her arms close together to protect her from the chill in the air.

"Okay, so what were we talking about?" Brandy asks as the girls move forward to cross the street onto campus. "Oh, yes, Nathan. That is so sweet. I can't believe he said that last night."

Penelope's face warms. "I really like him. I never thought I would feel this way about anyone so quickly. I'm just worried something is going to happen and ruin it all."

Brandy shakes her head. "I like him, too. Don't lose that one." She points at Penelope accusingly. "I don't care if he turns out to be a serial killer. Don't let that one get away."

They laugh out loud in the middle of the crosswalk, but inside, I'm not laughing. I would never let her near someone so dangerous.

I haven't discovered anything so dark as to reveal Nathan's serial-killer tendency, but I still have his ex-girlfriend to interview and that file. There is definitely something to uncover about his sister, Carol. I found nothing about his parents in the Better Business Bureau. They seem to run a tight, clean ship. No malpractice, no lawsuits, nothing.

Penelope tucks the hair that has blown over her left shoulder back behind her ear. "Well," she begins, coming down from her amused laughter, "I'm not worried about him being a criminal or anything. I just really want it to work out." She breathes in deeply, as if to savor a memory. "I just love the way he looks at me. I've never had anyone look at me that way before."

I look at you with even more adoration.

"And, last night, when he said he felt as if bumping into me changed his life, I wanted to tell him I knew exactly how he felt!" she exclaims her last words with a grunt.

That was an accident. He never should have had the chance. Her life wasn't supposed to change. It still hasn't, not drastically. There's still time to fix this.

"He says he doesn't want to see anyone but me," she adds. "He said, as far as he's concerned, I'm the only woman in the world. Funny thing is, that's how he makes me feel. When I'm with him, I really feel like the only woman in the world."

Brandy stops in her tracks, forcing the person behind her to quickly change route and dart around her. Penelope only slows a few steps ahead but turns toward her friend.

"My God," Brandy says dramatically before continuing to catch up to Penelope. "Why aren't you sleeping with him then?"

The back of Penelope's neck turns a pinkish shade of red, and her shoulders hunch. She puts her finger up to her lips. "Shh. Because," she says low, directing herself only to her friend and ignoring everyone else moving around her, "last night, we both decided we wanted to only see each other and see where it goes. So, we don't have any reason to rush it."

Penelope turns her face to the side where I can see her profile. She runs her tongue over her lower lip and then the top. "Not that I don't want to. Shit"—she bends her knees and pretends to melt—"he's so gorgeous. Those eyes. That face. His body." Her expression is like she's in a dream world, just thinking about him.

"You've got it bad," Brandy sarcastically drawls.

Penelope shakes her head. "You might be right. He wants me to go to dinner at his parents' house this Sunday."

My fists clench as we walk. I wonder if Carol Barker will be there. Maybe she's in jail. Maybe his family will have some explaining to do.

Thursdays, she has class on the other side of campus. Brandy will break off for her economics class in a few blocks. I'm not sure how much more I can hear before I get so angry, I punch something.

"So, where is he now?" Brandy asks.

Penelope sways as she walks. "He's out getting some stuff for his apartment. He wants drapes. The blinds in his place are kinda old and bent, so they don't move up and down anymore. He said he had a weird night last night when he went back to his apartment—like someone was watching him, or he had a dream someone was outside his place," she says with a hint of confusion in her voice. She turns to look at Brandy, grabbing even more of her attention. "He wanted me to tell you to keep a lookout for anything weird around our apartment building."

Brandy nods and agrees to be mindful but then reminds Penelope, "We live next to a campus; weird is the norm. Probably some drunk frat boys."

That's Brandy—always changing a heavy subject into a light one. *Good for her.*

"I'm sure you're right," Penelope agrees. "So, anyway, tell me more about bass boy." She sways her hips and lets them drift over to Brandy, smacking their sides together.

The girls giggle, and the sound makes me smile. I keep moving my head around, so no one picks up on the fact that they are making me smile with their conversation. When I move to the right, I see something that catches my eye.

Michelle is walking a path that moves diagonally across the parklike lawn area that runs in the middle of the Tafford campus. Her hair is down this morning, and her khaki peacoat is tied in a knot in front of her. She's looking down as she walks. If I call out to her, I wonder if she'll walk in the other direction. I certainly wouldn't blame her after the way I behaved last night.

I look back to Penelope and Brandy. We're almost to the building where Brandy has class. Penelope will be alone. It's my favorite time with her—when I feel like we're alone. My eyes travel back to Michelle, and I break away and tread across the faded green grass in her direction.

My hands go into my pockets as I get close. My chest feels heavy, and that sorrowful feeling that consumed me at times last night returns.

She looks up just as I utter her name. I said it softly so as to not scare her off.

Her eyes narrow, and she stops walking. Tilting her head to the side, she says, "Yes?"

She answered my call, but I have the feeling she was really saying, *What the hell do you want?*

I swallow hard, pushing down the bile rising in my throat. "I feel as if there's something I want to say to you, but I'm not going to be very good at saying it."

Michelle tilts her head to the other side, and the tension in her cheeks softens. "Why not?" she asks.

I look down and think about what to do with my body while talking to her. I'm feeling so uncomfortable and out of place. *Should I move my feet? Are my hands still okay in my pockets?* I breathe in slowly and forget about my mindless questions.

Looking back up to her caramel-espresso eyes, I tell her the truth, "Because I've never actually apologized before and meant it. I'm not sure if I'll do it justice."

A slow smile spreads her lips wider across her face. She tucks in her lips, trying not to smile so much so as not to tell me I'm forgiven.

"I am though," I add.

"What?" she asks, letting go of that smile she was holding back.

"Sorry," I simply say.

She exhales a deep breath, making the air around her mouth turn white. "I haven't had breakfast yet. Have you eaten?"

I nod. "I had an early start to the day. I ate at six this morning."

She glances down at her watch. "Nearly four hours ago. How about an early lunch?"

I would actually like that—a chance to sit down with her and attempt a better apology instead of standing here, rushing the words out before I'm on my way. If it's going to be my first real apology, it should be better than what I just did.

But I look up to Penelope walking alone. Brandy left for her class, and Penelope is only accompanied by the tree-lined paths. Michelle waits patiently for me to decide, and Penelope continues to walk farther away. Any moment now, she'll be out of sight.

Michelle looks down at her watch again, and one side of her mouth twists. "A really early lunch."

I fear she's about to give up on me.

This is my redemption, but I have a dilemma.

I look back to where Penelope should be, but her body has disappeared into the campus horizon.

"Yes," I say to Michelle, "I'd love to."

SIXTEEN

'm not terribly hungry, but I stand in line inside the student center anyway. Out of approximately ten, Subway is the only vendor who is serving breakfast and lunch at this hour. I must look ridiculously out of place, ordering a sandwich at ten in the morning. I scan the room, but nobody seems to be paying me any attention.

How do I blend in when I feel like I stick out like a sore thumb?

I prepare myself for the club, and the lights are so low, I can get away with a lot of imperfections.

Kevin used to be my research subject when it came to socializing during nightlife. I really don't like that guy, but I did learn a lot from him, and now, I feel as if I can mingle in the club in a comfortable way. But, in broad daylight, when I'm surrounded by people who are supposedly my peers, my nervousness about fitting in makes me forget how to behave in public.

I look over at Michelle, who is in line at the coffee stand. She belongs, at ease and natural in this environment. She leans to one hip and relaxes into it while she waits to move forward. I do the same as I wait in my line for a sandwich.

Although I haven't eaten anything in four hours, I did just have a coffee while waiting for Penelope at Aroma. It's enough to tide me over until a more appropriate lunch hour. But I watch Michelle and match her movements as she steps up in line. I'm studying her social cues, and it's worth the six dollars I'm going to waste on a sandwich.

Since she's become my subject to study and I'm mimicking her interactions with others, we end up walking away from our vendors at nearly the same time. I watch her expression as she looks at others, and I notice right away that it's different when she just wants to move past a person and how she looks at them when she notices something about them, like the fact that they're smiling at her. She smiles back. Sometimes, she initiates the smile.

I try the same and nod at a woman who nearly brushes my hip as she turns to the side to pass by me. She smiles back, like it's contagious. I make sure to notice if anyone smiles at me, and I return it.

Michelle and I meet at a booth in the back corner. She sets down her breakfast pastry and coffee while I place my wrapped sandwich on the table before sliding onto the long red bench. I don't bother unwrapping it yet; I'll wait until my appetite comes.

I watch as she takes her first bite. She pushes a crumb from the corner of her mouth into the center of her lips, so her tongue can reach out and catch it before it falls off.

"I lied to you," I blurt out.

Her head picks up, and she sits taller. "About what?"

About what? That's a good question. I think I have a million answers to it—most of them having to do with Kevin.

Baby steps. I remind myself to go slow with what I reveal.

Her elbows sit on top of the table, stretched out wide, and her hands lay flat in the middle. I copy her position, but since my arms are a lot longer than hers, my hands hover in the air a few inches from the table. It feels funny, so I bring my hands back down under the table. My stomach burns, feeling uneasy. Even if I hadn't had the coffee that ruined my appetite, I probably wouldn't be able to eat right now since I'm so uncomfortable in my vulnerability in this social situation.

"I'm not even close to being hungry right now." I push my still-wrapped sub further from me on the table.

Michelle brings both hands higher up and folds her fingers together, creating a triangle with her arms and her body. "Then, why did you agree to come with me here?" she asks.

"I told you, I wanted to apologize."

She seems to analyze my face, like the astute psychology student she is. "You already said you were sorry. Why are you really here?"

Because it didn't feel like it was enough, and now, I want to study your movements. Instead, I say, "Last night, you asked if we were friends."

She nods, remembering, and brings her coffee up to her lips for a taste.

"I can't imagine why you would want to be my friend."

She smiles at me softly and continues to eat her pastry.

This interaction is so much easier for her than it is for me, but at the same time, I admire her and want to learn from her interactions with other people, including me. Thus, I want to be around her more and will be making a point to see her more often.

I thought about Michelle a lot after I returned from Penelope and Nathan's apartment building last night. I wasn't able to get much sleep.

I can't stop thinking about how her forehead wrinkled in three places and her nostrils flared when she realized I was angry with her. *Is that her typical reaction when someone is upset with her, or was that just for me?*

"Alex, you're smart. Everyone on this campus knows you're pretty damn smart."

Not everyone, I say to myself, thinking about Penelope.

"I see the way you treat people; you're humble, and you're kind to those who treat others well. You have manners."

She eyes me playfully, making my chest feel tight with nerves.

How does she do that? Make her eyes scold me and play with me at the same time? I'll have to practice that in the mirror sometime.

"Those are great building blocks," she continues. "There's something about you that makes me want to know more."

"What if you don't like what you see? Like last night? I was an asshole to you last night." I wonder if she'll reveal something more about her reaction to my anger.

But she smiles and agrees, "Believe it or not, people make mistakes. Like I said, you have great building blocks even if the other stuff might need a little work."

She winks at me, and that knot I feel in my chest warms.

It makes me want to twitch my eye and practice winking at people—something I've never done before.

Her presence is making me feel more comfortable by the minute, knowing that she's now another subject for me to study. I expected more of a confrontation after yelling at her and leaving her in the December cold last night, but I feel welcome here. Just like how I feel at home when I'm in the lab. But this is a woman, and I've never felt comfortable interacting with a woman, not naturally like this. It doesn't seem logical, and it intrigues me.

"Do you still want to be my friend after the way I treated you last night?"

"Yes," she says quickly. "But, even more than that, I want to understand why you did it. What made you so angry?"

"You're the psychology major, so you tell me." My attempt at a joke works.

She opens her mouth with a smile, laughing through her nose. "I'm not a doctor yet."

I return her smile. "You will be. I'm not the only smart person on campus."

"Maybe not, but you're probably the only true genius." She takes the last bite of her pastry and grips her coffee cup in her hand. She flips her other wrist over to look at her watch. "I've gotta run to class. Do you want to talk about this more later today?"

I do. I want to talk to her more, period. But I wish I had a different answer for her. "Um, today's not good. I have some lab work to finish up, and then I have plans this evening."

"Right, finals are coming up. Everyone seems to get pretty busy around this time. Kevin even got up early this morning to study before heading to campus."

I hope he got up early for a shot of penicillin. Or worse, he stayed all night with the bartender.

Her shoulders slump, and I wonder if, deep down, she knows what I want to tell her about him.

She shakes whatever thought she has in her head and comes back to the present. "Okay then, another time." She grabs her bag from the seat and appears like she's going to walk away.

I should have been in the lab thirty minutes ago, but I feel the research I began here by studying Michelle is much more important to me.

"Wait," I say before she has a chance to leave. "How about tomorrow? Maybe you can join me for lunch at a more appropriate time?" My words come out dry, but I add a tight-lipped smile at the end. I don't want her to catch on to my ulterior motive for being around her.

She smiles back, much broader and comforting than mine, and nods. "Okay, tomorrow. How about here at noon?"

"Tomorrow then," I confirm.

SEVENTEEN

The concrete scent always stays the same, no matter how many years go by. The stairwell to the science labs is timeless and preserved with its simple solid steel structure.

I flip the switch, and the fluorescent lighting illuminates the room. My throne. Normally, I would set my briefcase on the usual stool and head to the lockers on the back wall. But I don't have my briefcase today.

I need one of her hair samples from my locker, and the key is always kept in my case. I'm about to curse for wasting my own time and leave the lab when I realize something. Without being able to sleep last night, I only had time to stop by my apartment and change shirts. Seeing Nathan made me so distraught, I walked around campus for hours.

I reach down to my right front jean pocket and pull out the lone strand of brilliant strawberry-blonde hair that I found at the club last night. When I pull it out, I remind myself it's in my fingers. I'm holding it and touching it. My research becomes that much more important to me.

This isn't happening so much in the name of science. This is something I'm doing to fill a need I have within myself. I *need* to hold and touch Penelope.

Originally, I was going to create the genetic code from scratch, but why mess with perfection?

This one is perfect—the hair I hold in my fingers. There's a round bulb at one end, telling me it's from the root. Everything I need is in that root.

Taking a test tube, I cut a small part of the hair off into the tube. That's all I need, yet it's so much; it's a whole person. The tube goes to the RapidHit DNA testing machine that was purchased by the university specifically for my work. As far as I'm concerned, I own it, and I don't allow anyone else to use it.

I punch in my authorization code, and the tester lights up for me.

The machine is no bigger than a printer. It takes forty-five minutes, and I have all the information I need from even the smallest of specimens. Nobody needs to know how I got the DNA; they just marvel at the scientific advancements I'm giving the world.

At the end of this semester, I'll be hearing about the progress on my approval for an artificial womb, created by Sci Gen Labs. I will literally be able to grow people in a lab. I'll be growing one specifically for me.

This kind of work would normally take someone years, for even the brightest in the industry. I'm different. What I've been setting out to accomplish, I can do in a matter of months. There has always been something different about me, something that sets me apart from the rest of the world. That's why I've never fit in with other people. Not unless they're my experiments, like Michelle.

A student comes and tries to open the door, but it's locked. They knock on the thick glass window for me to let them in, but I ignore them. This is my domain. I'm the only one who belongs here, and I have important work to do. Eventually, the student will give up. If he or she goes off to tell a professor, they'll tell him or her to fuck off, like I did. Everyone knows I practically own this place, even Dean Schumaker.

A muffled voice speaks to me, "It's locked. Can you let me in?"

Like the knocking, I just ignore it. The student can return another day when I'm busy with something else.

I could stay here and work my magic all night, but I make sure to leave the lab by eight o'clock. There's a long overdue appointment that I'd rather not miss.

EIGHTEEN

I've been coming here since my sophomore year of undergraduate studies, and nothing has ever changed. After I pass the receptionist at the front door, only a cover for this secret establishment, I take the elevator to the eleventh floor. It's there where the security becomes more intense.

Two private security guards stand outside when the elevator doors open. One stays at his post, and the other escorts me through two glass doors into a lounge area. The guard stands to the side of the couch while I approach Mrs. M.

She stands in her baby-pink tweed skirt suit. Long white pearls hang from her neck. If you didn't know any better, you would think she's a modern-day Chanel-wearing June Cleaver. But I know better. She's a high-class madam in disguise. Her business is possibly the best in the country. With all the politicians that filter in the area, she never worries about a lack of clientele. Other than long-term political staples, like the mayor and governor, I might be her most loyal customer. The privacy is worth every penny out of my heavy trust fund.

"It's so good to see you, Alex." She brings her dark-red-painted lips to pucker on each side of my cheeks. She's careful not to actually touch my skin and leave a smudge.

I kiss her on each side in return. "Mrs. M, you look beautiful, as always."

"Desiree is waiting for you in her room," she informs me. "Let me know if you ever feel like switching it up."

I give her a dry smile. "I like the consistency." My preferences are nobody's business, not even Mrs. M's.

"It's your hour." She politely nods her head, cueing me to proceed, before she returns to the couch and takes a seat.

The guard follows me down the hall to room 1103 and takes a professional stance with his back against the wall, just to the side of the solid dark wood door. Everyone in the building is escorted, and when a client is in session, the guard stands outside, listening for any screams alerting them to foul play. There's a safety word meant for the guard's cue to intervene. It's a tightly run establishment. Mrs. M doesn't make any mistakes. If she did, it would be one of the largest scandals in American history. Presidents have walked these halls...along with my father.

It's not required of me, but I knock to let Desiree know I'm entering her room.

She's just placing on her wig as I step across the threshold.

"You're a little bit early," she says, snapping her neck back and allowing the light-red hair to fall naturally around her face. She uses the tips of her fingernails to make small movements over her scalp, adjusting the wig into a comfortable place. "I was just finishing getting ready for you."

The color isn't perfect, but it works. It's enough for what I need from her here.

She walks over to me in her black lace thong and matching bra. I've never seen her in anything more.

"The usual again?"

"Yes," I confirm, taking my keys and wallet out of my back pocket and placing it on the long mirrored dresser against the wall. "But I'm actually in a time crunch. I need to be out of here a little earlier than usual." The library closes in just more than an hour. "I forgot something at my office. I need to pick it up before ten."

I sit down on the tufted bench at the end of the bed and bend down to take off my shoes. The dim lights are just enough to give a glowing candle effect. Although there is a window in the room, it's forbidden to open it, so it's covered by lush curtains.

Desiree readies herself and reaches into her thong, placing lubricant around the folds between her legs. After I take off my pants, I fold them and place them neatly on top of my T-shirt.

Before climbing onto the brown velvet-covered bed, I pull out my phone and the earbuds left in my jean pocket.

Desiree takes her usual position on her hands and knees in front of me. I remove her panties by pulling them around her curved ass and let them drop, so they loosely bind her knees together against the bed.

The sight of a woman's body—her curves not too different from Penelope's—with the vibrancy of light-red hair makes me instantly hard.

I take my hand and run it through her wig, titillating all my senses with thought. It's not real hair, but it's not hard to pretend. My thumb moves over my iPhone as I search for one of my recordings. I find the one I use for occasions like this, archived from ten months ago.

When the earbuds get placed in my ears, I press play. *Her* moans and sexual breathing put me in the moment, as if I were in the room with her.

I enter Desiree, thinking only of my sweet Penelope.

NINETEEN

I walk past students moving in herds in the other direction. It's not as if the number of people are causing this much of a crowd; it's just that the library only has a two-door exit to leave the building, and it is closing in less than five minutes.

I got caught up in enjoying my time with Desiree. It had been too long since I put my visions of being with Penelope in that way to life.

A young man bumps against my shoulder as he moves by me. "Sorry, man," I hear him call back to me.

I ignore the incident. I just keep moving forward to the hall in the midsection of the library and down to my office.

"The library is closing," someone informs me as I pass the checkout counter.

I nod but continue on my way. I just need my briefcase, and I'll be out with the rest of the students. I've put this off long enough.

I open my office door, grab my leather case, and leave just as quickly as I came.

My apartment door closes behind me, solidifying my solitude. But I'm not really alone. I have something in my hot little hand that will bring company to my thoughts.

I swing my briefcase up and let it fall onto my limestone kitchen countertop. The island is large and opens to the living room. It's never bothered me that the space doesn't hold a formal office. I don't spend enough time here to begin with, and when I do, I enjoy working at the large island.

Floor-to-ceiling windows give me enough backdrop of the campus and city to inspire anyone to enjoy living here. The Capitol building peeks its gold specks from the top of the dome through the other surrounding mid-rises.

I don't bother sitting. Pushing my case, tilting it toward me, I reach in to grab the manila file holding the documents that have been on my mind for two days.

Carol Barker's name runs across the tab on top in black ink. The Sacramento County Sheriff's Department's seven-point star emblem is still peeking out from the corner. I pull at it, sliding it out into the open.

It's a police report. Just over a year ago, Carol was involved in arson that caused her to go to the ER to be treated for burns. *This is interesting.* The report shows the crime happened on River Parkway. My eyes flash down to find Carol's address recorded, also on River Parkway. This saves me time in finding his parents' address.

Carol is five years younger than her older sibling. She's only a junior in high school.

Tsk, tsk, tsk, causing so much trouble.

It says here she attends Sacramento High. There might be even more interesting accounts in she school files. I wonder how often she breaks the law; surely, this can't be the first offense. It must have escalated to arson.

What I find most interesting about this report is that, even with all the damage recorded, no charges were filed. I wonder if her parents paid her victims off to cover something up. This is proof that Nathan and his family can't be as tame as he described to Penelope.

I set the police report to the side and fan through the other documents—a copy of her birth certificate, immunization and hospitalization records. A few years ago, she suffered from pneumonia and stayed at Mercy General for a week. I don't bother diving into more of her medical records. I don't care about her well-being. I just care about her secrets.

Grabbing an orange from the large bowl in the center of my island, I begin to peel it as I mull over my new discovery.

I look at the digital clock on the higher of the two stacked ovens—10:37. My jaw moves back and forth, as I consider if I should pay Penelope a visit tonight. I'd sleep much easier, knowing she's not currently spending her time with Nathan.

I pop a wedge of orange in my mouth, leaving the peel and remainder of the orange on the countertop. Grabbing my briefcase, I leave my apartment.

Just a quick peek, I tell myself after turning off my car.

I park in my usual spot in the lot at the end of Dalton Avenue.

First, I look up to Penelope's apartment. The lights are all off, and everything seems quiet, but I need to know for sure. I dig inside my briefcase and pull up the false bottom, exposing my listening devices. I insert my earbud plug into the side and tune into the channel where the bugs in her apartment will deliver any sound coming from her room.

I close my eyes and become one with the sound. One breath moves in and out, slowly and just audibly enough. I could almost drift off to sleep with her, but I can't make that mistake again. She's alone, which is all I really needed to know.

Satisfied, I move to turn my engine back on, but something stops me. It's a curiosity making me yearn to be closer. It's different from the pull I feel toward Penelope. This is driven by anger. It's almost as if I feel this intense need for revenge against him.

I get out of my car and start walking toward his apartment unit. Just being here last night and finding myself here again, I feel addicted to this new urge I feel.

The building is the same, the lawn in the back is the same, the pathway in front of the four doors are the same, but his unit has changed. In twenty-four hours, it's as if I were standing outside a different window. New blinds have been installed, and they're tilted down to a tight close, giving away nothing on the other side. In addition, there are curtains blocking any possible light that might escape through the unforgiving slats. It's the same for this living room window.

There's nothing for me here. I turn around and head back to where I came from.

Still on Dalton Avenue, on my way back to my car, headlights assault me from behind. I feel the lights slow as the car pulls up alongside me. I ignore the cop car as its driver-side window rolls down, obviously trying to intimidate me with his presence.

"Late night for a walk. Where are you heading?" Officer Smith asks from his slow-moving vehicle.

"That all depends on your perspective of time," I sarcastically say, my eyes straight ahead. I begin to cross the street to the parking lot where my car waits.

Officer Smith pulls his car around the street corner, blocking me from reaching the other side. "What are you doing out at eleven o'clock on the outskirts of a college campus?" he asks more assertively.

My hand flies up impatiently. "I'm walking to my car."

He takes an impatient breath, not caring to put up with my attitude. I cross the rest of the street by walking around the back of his car. When I reach the other side and step past the sidewalk to the lot, he rolls down the passenger window.

"Hey!" he yells. "I thought I told you I didn't want to see you parked there overnight."

I open my car door and pause before getting in to drive off. "Then, it's a good thing I'm leaving."

His frustration boils as I back my car out. But what can he do about it? Nothing but take notes, and I don't see a pen in his hand.

Perhaps this is how Kevin feels? Although Michelle and I are merely friends, I still feel like I'm juggling two women. Two research projects. Or maybe, in Michelle's case, it feels more like self-exploration.

Penelope is in her psychology discussion group, and Nathan is collecting next semester's assigned books from the student bookstore while he waits for her to be done.

"Hey, stranger," Michelle says behind me, standing at the end of the booth.

I've been staring out the window, watching the last stubborn leaf on a nearby campus tree finally give in to winter. The last of that glorious, vibrant color...until spring.

When I turn to greet Michelle, she notices the increased weight under my eyes. "You don't look like you're getting enough sleep," she observes, sliding into the booth, opposite me.

"Deadlines." An excuse.

Science is so clear to me. Even theories are based on facts. I can read, understand, and analyze DNA code like a librarian reads a children's book. It's simple and natural.

What's not natural is human nature.

"What are your plans after graduation?" I ask, wanting to change the subject from my sleep habits.

She smiles but shrugs. "Postdoctoral program. I'm thinking about applying for something here. I got my undergraduate degree in Washington. I like the California weather."

Me, too.

I brought the sandwich I never ate yesterday. I wait to unwrap it until after she's done speaking. I didn't want anything distracting me from listening to her answer my question.

"So, what did you do last night?" Michelle asks, a clear attempt at a new topic.

Again, it's not something I want to discuss.

"I was in the lab. How about you?" Lying to her seems wrong, but it's necessary.

"Kevin and I studied at my place," she answers. "Finals are next week. I feel ready, but there's always more you can do before finals. I'm looking forward to next semester. Aren't you?"

I want to say yes, but that would be a lie. I've already lied to her twice in the few minutes we've had together. These have been simple questions, but they feel hard for me to answer.

"The semesters all feel the same to me. I earn credits in a non-traditional way, so I don't attend lectures. It's all the same," I repeat. That's about as honest of an answer as I can give.

She places her elbows on the table and leans into her hands. "Maybe you're not challenging yourself enough."

I scoff. *Does she know who I am?* "Yesterday, you said I was a genius, the smartest man on campus," I remind her and make a point not to argue her previous statement.

She nods, taking a bite of her lunch. "Just because you're smart doesn't mean you're challenging yourself. You need to do something outside of your comfort zone."

My hands fall in my lap, and I watch her eat, watch her move flawlessly through this lunch meeting and the conversation we're trying to have. She looks up with her caramel-espresso eyes and softly smiles while chewing.

"You make me uncomfortable," I confess. "I'm looking forward to spending more time with you next semester."

Her chewing slows, but her eyes don't avert from mine. After swallowing, she tilts her head slightly to the side, something I've observed she does when she's analyzing something.

When she doesn't say anything, my discomfort increases, and I fight the urge to squirm in my seat. My hands remain in my lap, hidden under the tabletop, but they twitch, wanting so badly to come up and let my teeth chew on my fingernails.

"I don't have many friends," I try to further explain myself, maybe in a way that might make her feel more at ease.

"Kevin is your friend," she retorts.

No.

I say nothing. Again, I don't want to lie to her.

"What do you see in him?" I ask instead.

She softly runs her bottom teeth over her top lip. "I'm still figuring things out with him, but he seems really well rounded."

Wrong.

"I don't have any reason not to continue seeing him, so I guess that's what I see in him."

"Sounds like you're not challenging yourself enough."

She breathes in sharply as she sits up straighter, ignoring her food. I've clearly offended her.

"Have you ever been in a relationship, Alex?"

Yes. I have Penelope.

Michelle would never understand the depths of my connection with her. My love, commitment, and the desire to put her needs before mine. But there is no one else I can mention who would satisfy Michelle.

I swallow hard, not wanting to lie to her again, but I do. "No."

"They're complicated."

"It's not that complicated, Michelle. Either there are good qualities to enjoy or bad qualities to walk away from. Seems very black and white to me."

Kevin falls under the category of bad quality, and she needs to walk—no, run away from him.

She reaches across the table, but there's nothing for her to reach for. My hands remain in my lap. It's not just her hands reaching across, but also her eyes dive into me.

"Alex, someone's best quality is also their worst. It's the most extreme parts of us that are extraordinary but can also be very unrelatable."

For some reason, I have this feeling we're not talking about Kevin. She's looking at me like she's telling me something about myself.

My stomach swirls with discomfort. I don't feel angry, just uneasy. And I realize…she's challenging me.

TWENTY

River Parkway is on the outskirts of the Sacramento city boundaries. The homes on the west side of the street, like the Barkers', have an expansive valley beyond their backyards.

The homes here were built on large lots in the early 1900s. With the continued growth of wealth in this section of town, I think it's safe to assume they have all been remodeled. They appear modest from the outside, but inside is likely charm mixed with high-end finishes. I've done my research.

I pass 954 River Parkway—the home Carol nearly burned to the ground and got away with. I don't see any leftover damage. The repairs must have been made quickly after the assault.

I keep driving down the block, farther from the house. If either Penelope or Nathan noticed my car after I set the alarm off last month, they won't have the chance to recognize it here. There's only one way into the neighborhood, and there's no reason for them to drive past his parents' house to where I plan to park.

Making my way toward the Barkers' house, I admire the area, comparing it to mine. I never had neighbors. At least not without gates, fences, and trees fending off visitors. There's no privacy here.

The Barkers' home has a wide front porch that expands across the entire front. The window frames are outlined with green trim while the rest of the house is yellow-painted siding and brick. It seems modest, even the landscaping, but it's impeccably kept, like all the others on the block.

The porch lights are off at the home next door, so I scope out a spot where I can get a good view into as much of Nathan's childhood home as possible. I can hide myself among the leaves of the untrimmed bushes and give myself a decent view of both the kitchen and dining room. Around the back is a field where I can move to if they decide to chat in the family room.

The lights in their home will blind them to the dark evening, becoming darker as the minutes pass. I'll be well hidden.

Penelope and Nathan arrive on his motorcycle, making my anger rise into my chest.

At least she's safely here, I remind myself, calming my temper enough to remain still within the leaves.

After she dismounts his crotch rocket, Nathan lifts a compartment and pulls out a bottle of wine. He hands a bouquet of roses and stargazer lilies wrapped in brown paper to Penelope. She looks nervous but not enough to hesitate. Carrying the bouquet, she walks up to the front door. My girl looks so brave, taking a deep breath before Nathan opens the door without knocking.

The moment the door is swung open, Nathan announces their presence, and shrieks from Mrs. Barker travel from the kitchen to the entrance. Her body isn't far behind her calls of excitement.

"It's so nice to meet you, dear," I hear as the door closes behind them.

All I can hear are murmurs until their lips become visible as they congregate in the kitchen.

"Is there anything I can help with?" Penelope says, handing the bouquet to Mrs. Barker.

I don't catch her response because she turns her back once she takes the bouquet. A man, who I assume is Nathan's father, walks into the scene. Young Nathan must have gotten his jet-black hair from his mother, but his stature and blue eyes mirror his father in the kitchen.

Penelope moves her hand out to shake his. "It's so nice to meet you," she tells him.

Mr. Barker laughs at her hand and opens his arms.

Nathan's mother is leaning over the sink, filling a vase with water. I have a perfect, direct view of her lips moving.

"So, this is the girl who made you drop your phone while you were chatting with me?" She has such a content smile on her face, as if her world were complete now that these people are filling her home.

The small talk continues until Nathan taps his mother on the shoulder. "Where's Carol?" he asks.

I expect the mention of the troubled teen to cause tension in the family, but nothing seems to change.

"In the living room," she informs him. This reminds her of something. She reaches for his forearm before she loses his attention. "Oh, and the Pendletons will stop by later."

Pendleton...that's the name of the victims from the arson two years ago.

Nathan turns to Penelope with an excited look on his face. "Come on, I want you to meet my sister."

This should be good.

I take a chance and step back from the bushes, moving closer to the neighboring house. Walking along the length of the home, I make my way to the backyard. Although most of the trees are bare, the valley in the back of their home is lush with tall, dry grass.

By the time I make it to a secure place to see into the living-room window, they've all interacted enough to be comfortable with each other. Penelope is laughing at something Nathan's father said, but his mother prompts them to cover their eyes with their hands.

They're playing a game, and I don't see Carol anywhere.

"Okay, we're all ready," Mrs. Barker says animatedly, her hands still over her face.

A figure in a black-and-red uniform with matching pom-poms moves from down the hall, becoming clearer as it nears the large lit room.

"Surprise!" Carol jumps up from behind the couch Penelope and Nathan are sitting on and waves the pom-poms in the air.

Every family member turns to excite over her entrance.

Her rounded belly decreases her ability for strength and stability in her midsection, aiding in her incoordination. Yet she focuses on every move she makes. They are simple hand and foot movements, but she takes them so seriously.

I have my suspicions from seeing her from afar, but from what I can tell, Carol has Down syndrome. I should have read her entire file.

I sink into the sod, letting the crunching sound of breaking grass echo around me. Carol isn't a delinquent at all. There could be several explanations for the fire. All of them would likely conclude to being an accident.

Breathing heavily out of my nose, I feel as if the force were moving the air around me like a bull ready to charge.

I have nothing. Nothing to draw Penelope away from Nathan and his family.

I peek back into the window and see the warmth they exude toward each other. Penelope is swimming in it, and she looks beautiful. Happiness looks so good on her.

Carol stands, facing Penelope while she sits on the couch.

She reaches out to hold Carol's hands and tells her, "I think you make a beautiful cheerleader."

I can't see Carol's response, but I do see how Nathan and his parents look at Penelope. She fits right in with them. And they want her. They want to take her away from me. My hand reaches up, and my fingers find enough length in my hair for me to pull until it hurts. My throat feels as if a rock were stuck inside. I can't make the feeling move up or down; it's just stuck.

She's slipping through my fingers.

I move back to my first position to watch them eat dinner together. All of them sit around the table, passing plates of food, laughing, talking, and touching each other. Penelope sits next to Nathan, and his left arm is hidden under the table at just the right angle for me to know that his hand is on Penelope's thigh.

Mrs. Barker leans into her left side and says, "Dear, what are your plans for Christmas?"

"I usually go home and spend the break with my mother. But"—she looks over to Nathan and smiles up at him before turning back to his mom—"Nathan and I were talking about spending most of the time on campus. Maybe doing something on New Year's Eve together."

"So, it's just you and your mother?" Mrs. Barker asks.

Penelope nods.

Nathan steps in to explain, "Penelope's dad passed away when she was younger."

Her head tilts to the side with sympathy. "Oh, dear, I'm so sorry."

Penelope just nods, shy from the attention on the subject.

"Well"—Mrs. Barker's hand moves to rest on Penelope's forearm—"we would love if you and your mother could join us for Christmas."

My girl lowers her head ever so slightly and blushes. She turns to look at Nathan and studies his reaction. He nods, approving, an eager smile on his face.

When Penelope turns her head away, Nathan looks to his mother, as if to say, *Thank you.*

"I am flattered that you've offered. I can't make any promises, but I will definitely talk to my mother about it."

Of course, her mother would want to join the Barkers for the holidays. It would be a flashback to her previous life, a break from the stress of cooking while attending medical school, and most importantly, a chance to see whom her daughter is associating with.

I only have eight days to put a stop to Nathan before her mother comes to meet, in her mind, the future in-laws. This is getting way too serious, too fast.

After dinner, an older couple from two doors down comes over with a plate of cookies. The empty-nesters come to pay Penelope a visit and see for themselves how wonderful of a girl she really is. As always, she doesn't disappoint. The Pendletons are treated like family within the Barkers' home.

I wonder if the incident with Carol occurred because they are friends, close enough for something like that to happen during a weekly visit, or if the fire was destiny that brought the two families closer together. Nobody would have blamed the Pendletons for hating the family who had caused so much trouble in their lives. But, as I watch them interact now, they clearly don't.

"Penelope and I should get going. We're meeting some friends out," Nathan says to his parents and neighbors.

I pull out my phone, turn down the screen brightness to as low as possible, and send a text to Kevin.

Alex: Meet me at the club tonight.

His reply comes within seconds.

Kevin: Michelle is with me.

Alex: Bring her.

A calm warmness in my belly begins to spread throughout my insides and loosens that rock sitting in my throat. The thought of seeing Michelle again makes me feel good, hopeful even. I'm

123

beginning to feel as if she might actually enjoy my company as much as I enjoy hers.

Getting to know her lately, I'm starting to feel a sense of responsibility toward her. The kind of responsibility a friend would have toward another—to be loyal.

Kevin will be on his best behavior while she's around. That will at least put off the inevitable pain she'll feel when she eventually learns who he really is.

The rock in my throat returns when I see Penelope swing her leg over Nathan's bike.

TWENTY-ONE

There was a moment in the kitchen when Mr. Barker was helping his wife with the dishes.

"He thinks she's the one," she told her husband.

How the hell could he know that?

He doesn't even know her. He doesn't know the mole on her collarbone and how four other freckles surround it when she's spent too much time in the sun. He doesn't know she picks up a twang when she spends more than an hour with someone who has a thick Southern accent. He couldn't possibly know that she and her mother pick up flowers from the same street vendor on the way to her father's resting site every year.

What does he know?

Only I know these things because I'm the only one who truly loves her and takes care of her. I've been doing it for years.

I sit in my car, waiting and watching the front entrance for Kevin and Michelle to show up, but Penelope and Nathan beat them to it. I consider going inside without my wingman, but I stop myself. Watching other students, some younger and some who look like they can be my peers, I wonder if I fit in. That's why I need Kevin; he gives me a place in that bar. But I don't look that different from the other people going inside. I dress the same, copy their mannerisms, and act appropriately for the scene.

Fuck Kevin, I say to myself just in time to spot Michelle holding his hand and walking into the club.

I catch up to them just inside the dim bar with black walls.

"Let's check out the bar on the right," Kevin says after spotting the bartender he slept with at her usual post.

Michelle doesn't argue, so neither do I. Right now is neither the time nor the place to expose Kevin for who he really is. I came to be here with someone else.

"Just a beer," I say once we reach the barstools.

Looking down to the main floor, I spot Penelope and Nathan. They're talking with Brandy and whom I recognize as the bass player from last week's show. I wonder if Brandy came here with him or if she just met him here. Either way, they seem close enough for me to assume they're committed to being near each other all night.

"Do you know them?" Michelle asks close to my ear.

I didn't realize I was staring long enough for anyone to notice.

"No," I tell her. "I must have zoned out. I wasn't really looking at anything in particular."

"She's pretty," Michelle says and points her glance toward where Penelope is.

I give Michelle a stern look. "I wasn't looking at anyone in particular."

She rolls her eyes and shakes her head. "Okay, Alex. Didn't mean to offend you." She grabs her beer from the countertop and moves to the other side of Kevin, further from where I'm sitting.

The rest of the evening, I make a point not to look at Penelope. Michelle is too observant and the only person who has ever really seemed to pay attention to me enough to notice anything.

Since I'm not able to focus all my attention on Penelope, I think a lot about where Michelle and Kevin are and what they're doing. Still, at least I know where Penelope is.

Whenever Michelle looks away or the one time she left us both to go to the restroom, Kevin takes the opportunity to make advances toward a blonde in a short dress. Since he spotted her, I've noticed he's been less affectionate toward Michelle. He has his blinders on and is after another victim for a notch on his bedpost.

I would have thought he would be able to show a little more restraint when his girlfriend was with him.

Scum of the earth.

Penelope and Brandy are enjoying dancing with each other and their dates. I taste the last warm sip of my beer when Michelle moves to sit near me again, and Kevin turns to order another drink.

"What's gotten into you tonight? You seem a little moodier than usual."

I keep my gaze down, not moving after she spoke, as if her presence didn't affect me. "So, I'm moody."

Kevin turns, still leaning as far over the bar as his upper body will allow, and taps my shoulder. I nod, knowing he's asking if I want another round.

"You don't have to try to be difficult," Michelle pipes up. "You just seem moodier than you need to be."

I don't answer, and I give nothing away as a response. I just stare out onto the crowded dance floor. It's a mass of people, but I see *her*. She stands out, as if a spotlight were shining upon her, but it's just my familiarity with her that makes her so vibrant and obvious to me.

Michelle shifts, frustrated with me for some reason. "Rough day in the lab?" she asks, obviously searching for some sort of explanation for my reluctance to indulge in conversation.

I grab the cold beer that was passed down to me, tilt one eyebrow, and take a sip. "I guess you could say that. I was surprised by something today—let down. I'm not used to being wrong." I turn and look up to her standing by my side. "About anything. I don't care for it."

She considers what I said and shifts uncomfortably. "Maybe you need to be wrong before you can be right. Isn't that the point of experiments?"

I shake my head, back to focusing on the dance floor. Without raising my voice, I just state to the air in front of me, "That is the dumbest fucking thing I've ever heard."

I regret it as soon as the words have left my mouth. Quickly, I turn to see her reaction and am met with a look on her face that tells me the extent of the damage I've done.

She moves to the other side of me and grabs Kevin's attention. "You know, it's been a long night. I'm gonna head home."

I can see the wheels turning inside his head, imagining he's thinking, *Good idea. I'll just stay here and fuck someone.*

"Okay, sweetheart. I don't think Alex is ready to leave yet, so I'll stay back with him." The grin on his face widens. *He's using me?* "I'll call you in the morning."

Michelle sighs—because of me or Kevin, I'm not sure. They turn away from each other, and Kevin wastes no time in making eye contact with the slutty blonde.

When she moves past me, I almost let her walk off, but I reach out and catch her hand just before it leaves my reach.

Her head whips around to see my hand holding her back.

"You can do better than Kevin."

"What?" she asks, moving her eyes from me to Kevin and then to the woman he's making faces with. "What are you saying?"

"Do you want me to tell you, or do you want to figure it out on your own? You're my only friend."

She looks confused by my statement, and she narrows her eyes down on me.

"I don't know what the right thing to do is."

"I need to go." She yanks her arm free and storms off.

Kevin doesn't even care to see her out the door. He's already moving from his seat with the intention to pounce on the blonde near the dance floor.

It's out of my hands now. It's her problem.

Still sitting here on a barstool, I notice a lot of people around me. Everyone is pushing around, fighting for more space and the bartender's attention. Even with so many people in a room, you can still be alone. *So much for having a wingman.*

Kevin and Penelope are on opposite sides of the dance floor. Penelope is with Nathan and Brandy. They're smiling and having fun, moving around and letting off steam before finals begin. Kevin is moving around his blonde, as if it were a sexual ritual. It's only a matter of moments before they go off somewhere to consummate the ceremony he's performing in the middle of the club.

I just sit and sip my beer, knowing I can't do anything to stop the inevitable.

"I think I knew but didn't want to believe the worst." Michelle's voice brings hope into the night.

I look up to find her standing just behind my left side, watching just as I was.

I stand up to meet her eyes. "Michelle, I'm sorry."

She breathes in slowly and turns her head for more strength to control the tears wanting to burst out of her eyes. She sniffles and turns back to look at me, trying to smile. "It's okay. He's a jerk. I just feel stupid."

"I think you're the smartest woman I've ever spoken to. I've learned from you." Air puffs out of my mouth, and I force a fake laugh. "And I'm a genius."

Michelle wants to chuckle at what I just said, but the movements to her mouth release the tension she was holding on to, and she begins to cry. She leans into me and wraps her arms around my midsection, letting her tears soak my shirt.

With all the loud music surrounding me, all I can feel is her heartbeat near mine. I still haven't moved my arms. I don't know how long she'll be like this. She seems comfortable. *If I move, will it disturb her or comfort her?*

Slowly, my hands move up and cross each other on her back. I press them down. Once, I apply a little pressure, and I can feel her weight move and almost meld into mine.

Her head rests just under my chin, and I can feel her soft brown hairs tickle my jaw. I begin to breathe in just as slowly as she does. For a moment, I feel as if we're one.

My right hand moves up, and I brush her hair through my fingertips. Heat rises in my throat, and I feel almost satiated with the touch of something so soft and satisfying.

When she feels well enough to stand on her own, she slowly pulls away from me. "Sorry."

I shake my head. "Don't be sorry." There are a million things running through my mind, but that was the only thing I could think to say.

She looks past me, and I turn to see what's caught her eye. Kevin is taking the blonde's hand and leading her away from the dance floor, out the back. Michelle sniffles again and uses her knuckle to wipe moisture away from under her eye.

"Bye, Alex," she says and then moves to turn and leave. After a step away from me, she turns back and adds, "Thanks for the heads-up."

Then, she's gone.

My chest aches at the thought of her pain. Kevin isn't worth it, but that doesn't seem to matter to me. It's not logical, but it's real. I saw it on her face, and I would have given anything to take it away.

I sit back down on my barstool, not noticing the sound or movements around me. My mind is quiet, except for thoughts about what just transpired with Michelle. *Could I have prevented her pain or at least controlled it? I should have been protecting her, too, not just Penelope.*

Breaking out of my trance over Michelle, I look up and scan the room for my beautiful Penelope. She's gone. They all are. There's no sight of Brandy, her bass player, or Nathan. I was too distressed over Michelle to notice her leaving.

I look around at everyone drinking and enjoying themselves. There's nothing for me here.

Feeling confused and deterred, I stand up to leave. I'll go home and get the much-needed sleep my body's been craving for weeks.

TWENTY-TWO

Strawberry-blonde bounces with her trot twenty feet ahead of me. Nathan's predatory gait keeps up with her, and he attaches himself to her body by holding her hand.

Brandy finished her last final yesterday, so she left for home then. She'll be celebrating the holiday with her family in Denver.

Penelope is bordering late for her nutrition class final. It's a happy trot, knowing she'll do just as well on this test as she has on all the others this week.

Nathan brings her hand up to his lips and kisses it as they move along. "Excited about Christmas?" he asks.

Penelope nods excitedly. "Are you sure your parents are okay with me and my mom joining you?"

He chuckles a little, as if her question were silly. "Growing up, we always had room for more at our dinner table. My parents believe the more, the merrier." I can see his thumb rub across the top of her hand. "Plus, it just feels right."

She abruptly stops walking, forcing him to stop with her. Still holding his hand, she asks, "Do you worry we're moving too fast?"

Nathan swallows and takes time to really think about her question. He lowers his head, closer to hers. "No, I don't. I'm not sure I could slow down even if I wanted to."

Her chest moves up and down as I slow my walk, passing them along with the other students on the campus path. "I feel the same way," I hear her say.

"I-I..." Nathan struggles with his next words. His voice begins to trail off in the distance, but I can hear him tell her, "We should get you to class. I'm not gonna let you be late for your final."

I'm walking ahead of them, and there's not much I can do about it now. I know where she'll be, so I bank left and head past the psychology hall, going toward the science building where my lab is.

My research is beyond Professor Whitaker's comprehension. I just handed him the future of genetic science on a silver platter, not that he can take any credit for it. He's merely a background figure, placed there for aesthetics and balance in the academic world.

As I pass by the psychology hall on my way out, I see Michelle exit the building. I pause, and she slows when she sees me but still descends the stairs to where I am.

She stops two feet away from me and adjusts the book-bag strap over her shoulder.

It takes a while before either of us speaks. I'm not sure what to say to her after last weekend. I didn't reach out. *Should I have?*

Kevin texted me three times, but I ignored every one. I understand that she isn't speaking to him, and he's trying to get her back. But he also sent a message saying he needed to get laid and wanted to go to the club. Whether he did or not, I'm not sure. I won't let him use me anymore—and certainly not as an accomplice to help him hurt Michelle.

"Lunch?" Michelle asks, finally saying something.

I nod, and we begin walking together.

"I hate winter." I'm trying to open up and say something that might make her engage with me. There's no motive, no need, other than to just talk with her, and it feels strange, challenging even.

"You don't like the cold?"

I shake my head. "It's not that. I don't mind the temperature. It's the dryness that sucks away all the color. The leaves don't even want to hang on to their lifeline anymore." I pull a bare branch on a tree as we walk by it. The branch springs back after I let go.

"I've always appreciated the natural cycle of the seasons." She shakes her head, disagreeing with a thought that entered her mind. "The leaves aren't abandoning their life source. It's the tree that needs to let go of the past, so it can flourish in the spring. They become more beautiful every year. It's about growth."

This woman astounds me with her perspective.

"How do you do that?" I ask.

"What?"

My briefcase swings between us as we continue to walk.

"Make me feel like I'm not the smartest man in the room." Or the outdoors, where we are, but I'm confident Michelle understands what I'm trying to say.

She laughs through her nose, like she often does. "You're still the smartest man in the room, Alex. I'm a woman." She looks up to me with devious confidence and a hint of feminism.

Her quip makes me smile. "See, you've done it again."

As we near the student center, I feel like I want to share even more with her. Explain to her that my feelings toward winter aren't just science-based—obviously, or I'd know every fact—but a reason behind my emotional reaction to the season.

"I used to garden with my mother when I was a little boy."

"And that's why you like the spring." She understands. "Are you close with your mom?"

The thought of my mother and the betrayal I feel toward the lie of my upbringing makes my jaw tighten. "I was," I say sharply so as to put an end to the subject.

After we enter the student center, we go our separate ways until we return to our usual booth with our food.

I arrive at the booth first, so I look out the window and wait until she joins me.

"What was your favorite flower to plant?" Michelle asks from my side, holding her tray. "When you were a boy and you gardened…what was your favorite?" She slides in across from me.

My mouth moves into a smile as I remember how much I enjoy them. "Poppies."

She beams, as if she had never been hurt before. As if life had never pained her. As if I had never let Kevin cheat on her for so long because of my own selfish motives.

"The state flower—interesting. What do you like so much about them?"

I tilt my head, as if I were leaning on my thoughts. A habit I might have picked up from her. "Their simple beauty and elegance. The way the petals hold themselves up and show off the simplicity of their vibrant color." I almost become lost, thinking about the joy and serenity it brings me.

My gaze moves to melt into hers. One moment, I'm daydreaming of orange liveliness dancing in my mind, and the next, I'm drowning in a pool of caramel espresso.

"How are your tests? Are you happy with your semester?" I want to talk more about her.

"Yes. I'm done now," she says with a straight face. She begins eating her food, as if it tasted bad, but she swallows it anyway. Her attention is solely on the plate in front of her. "Looking forward to moving on though."

Kevin. She's talking about moving on from Kevin. Putting him in the past with her classes.

"I'm sorry about Kevin." I wait to see a reaction from her, but she continues to focus on eating her food. "I meant what I said…you can do so much better."

She gives a curt nod with tight lips.

Is she angry with me? Does she know it's all my fault that he deceived her for so long?

"I'm sorry," I say again.

She drops her fork, creating an echo after the clatter. "Why are you apologizing so much to me when, apparently, you've never even done it until recently?" Her hands fall in her lap, and she sits back, patiently waiting for a response.

I don't move or speak. I don't have an answer for her—at least, not one that will satisfy her.

Tired of waiting for me to say anything, Michelle flutters her eyes up. "Anyway," she goes on to say, "it's not your fault he's an asshole."

I look to each side of me, searching for inspiration in my environment. But I look ahead to my real inspiration and draw strength. "Maybe so, but I could have told you before I did."

My hand trembles under the table, wanting to come up and reach across to touch hers, but I resist, knowing it's too intimate. More than what I can handle.

She considers my words. "Technically, you didn't tell me. You just gave me the option to find out on my own or to read into your obvious warning." Her soft smile tells me I'm forgiven.

A rock forges and bonds in my throat. "Can I tell you something?" I earnestly ask her.

She places her elbow on the table and leans in closer to absorb whatever it is I'm about to reveal. "Of course."

The rock remains in my throat as I breathe past it, feeling it in my way. "I care about you. And, because I care about you, I know I should have protected you from Kevin."

She exhales a breath she was holding since before my confession. "It's not your fault. You can't control everything. You can't control people." She punches out her sentences, as if she were frustrated that I didn't already know this.

I bring my hands up to the table, giving me more stability.

"Alex"—she reaches across the table and puts her hand over mine—"you weren't born my friend. You couldn't have known where the line was until you did. I'm grateful you said something, period. You're not responsible for that asshole's actions." She leans back and picks up her fork. "End of story."

There is something so warm in my body when I watch her speak. It's not a sexual attraction. Although she's become something so beautiful to me. It's just unexplainably warm. It starts in my chest and then moves to the rest of my body.

I look away, not wanting to face how I feel at the moment, and spot Penelope walking along one of the campus paths. She must have finished her final early.

Attagirl.

I begin to scoot out of the booth. "Michelle, I'm sorry. I need to leave."

Her brows crease, and her palm turns up and moves over the table. "But you've barely touched your lunch."

Continuing to scoot, I think of how it would feel to be behind Penelope as she walks alone. As if we were walking alone. I need to be with my girl.

Standing, I look down on Michelle. "I'll talk to you over break," I tell her.

She looks out the window and possibly sees the lone, beautiful girl walking across campus yards away from the student center.

"You don't have to leave," she states after looking back to me.

"I do. But I'll reach out soon. I'll be here for break, so when you get back to campus, I'd love to see you."

She breathes in, deep and slow, putting off the inevitable—my departure. "Fine," she says curtly, letting me go without further debate. "I'll see you later. I'll be back on Wednesday." She turns to look back out the window in Penelope's direction and allows me the emotional space to leave.

TWENTY-THREE

That son of a bitch.

I sit in my car in the parking lot at the end of Dalton Avenue where I like to see the light in her room. The last glimpse of daylight has just fallen beyond the horizon. There is a clear statement of darkness that declares nighttime.

All light and inhibitions become dim, absent even.

Nathan is taking advantage of the early dark sky. Both of their hearts pound, and their blood fills their veins with anticipation as they create the creak in each step on their way up to her apartment.

The kiss they shared moments ago was only foreplay. I can't set off my car alarm now. At best, it would only scare them into her apartment together. I scramble to put my earbuds into my ear sockets and ready myself to listen to what I know deep down is the inevitable.

They don't waste any time. My groin aches with a pain, as if I just got kicked. Her moans don't turn me on. They don't make me feel good. Her pleasure has nothing to do with me. The sound of her heavy breathing and panting only make that sickening feeling that started in my groin grow.

How could she do this to me?

This is all his fault. He is the unknown in this equation. The one who inserted himself where he wasn't wanted. Where he doesn't belong.

I can't help but listen, like a car crash that everyone slows down to watch. It's not something they actually want to see. It's not something they even planned on seeing. It's just the hard, unforgiving truth that they can't deny, and once they know it exists, they can't help but witness it so that they know the unbelievable isn't just in their imagination.

My body convulses. I punch the leather seat next to me, followed by the steering wheel in front of me, and I kick the underbelly of the dashboard. Anything. I just want to hurt, punch, and hit anything within my reach when her moans begin to escalate.

My jaw clenches, and my teeth gnash, as if I were tearing something apart.

Turn it off! I scream at myself inside my head.

But I can't. I can't seem to make a move to ease my pain. I have to know, and I have to hear it.

She is mine, I remind myself. *She is mine.*

Tears begin building within my sinuses, wanting to push out of my eyes. I resist the pressure that's building. I can feel the blood vessels popping with my strength. With the moans I hear her calling and the exciting, pleasurable sounds that she sings, I just grunt, wanting to push the pain and the noise out of my mind.

It all comes to a climax. I cry as I hear her call out, releasing her orgasm. My flow of tears release into raging rapids of emotion once I realize that Nathan is coming with her.

This isn't mine. My heart aches.

But, once I feel that heavy thud of each rhythmic beat of my heart, a realization hits me. I've been too distracted with my friendship with Michelle. I need to do what's right for Penelope even if she doesn't realize it herself. I need to get rid of Nathan. I need to do it now.

I can't let what happened to Michelle happen to Penelope. I can't let *her* get hurt. I could never forgive myself. Nathan is the one who needs to suffer. Carol Barker is going to have to take the blame, but at least I'll be saving my Penelope from the inevitable.

I wish I had more time to plan everything. I can't say it's foolproof or that there is any guarantee there won't be a proper investigation once it's over. But, if it all goes as planned, Carol Barker will be the arsonist, just as she was two years ago.

I picked up a pair of Sacramento High pom-poms. The same set she already owns. If I find the right opportunity, I'll set them outside, hoping the originals burn in the fire. I'll just set the fire to the exterior of the home and hope they assume she came outside. Hopefully, Carol has some underlying fascination with fire that can easily be blamed for the blaze I'm destined to set.

There hasn't been enough time to fully think this through, but I'm feeling desperate for instant results.

Waiting in the field at the back of the home, I notice nobody is in the living room by the sliding glass door leading outside. I move to get closer to the house with the pom-poms and box of matches. As I'm wearing all black with my hoodie pulled over my head, it'll be very hard for someone from inside the lit home to see me.

I set up at the back corner, closer to the rear of the home where the valley seems to meet the residence. I'll need to do this quickly since I'm exposed around the corner of the neatly landscaped yard.

After putting on my latex gloves, I hold up the matchstick and look at it as if it were my friend. *This is for trying to take her away from me.* I strike it against the side of the house and listen to the crackle that speaks to me when the heat fights to explode from the little accelerant put on the stick. Feeding on the oxygen around it, it steadily grows to an elongated teardrop shape with an orange-and-yellow glow.

I hold the small fire on a stick close to the siding, allowing the heat to scorch the yellow paint and dig deeper to the wood panels. It burns, leaving a black residue, but doesn't develop enough to be an independent flame on the side of the house. I knew it wasn't going to catch after one. I'm not sure how many I'll need to use. I shake the tiny bit of stick left in my hand and wave out the spark before it burns through the latex on my fingertips.

I take out another stick to ignite it, but the wind picks up at the most inopportune time for the fire to light. I drop the dud to the ground and pull out another, but I stop before I have a chance to strike another one against the home. Over the rustling of dry grass in the wind, I can hear the rumbling of Nathan's motorcycle.

They're here already? It's only three.

Maybe it's just Nathan, and Penelope is giving him space to be with his family alone before she arrives. I leave the pom-poms where they are and move further down the side of the house where

I can hide in the foliage and still have a view of the front. I need to figure out who's going to be entering the home. If Penelope is anywhere near here, I'll have to put off my plan.

Nathan appears to be alone on his bike. Once the noise from the motorcycle calms to a quiet, he pulls out another bottle of wine but stands on the sidewalk, not moving toward the house. He looks around, and I wonder what the hell he's looking for.

The front door swings open, and Carol comes running out of her house. "Natey!" she yells.

Nathan's face instantly lights up. Carol runs right up to her brother with the excitement of a puppy. He matches her enthusiasm but remains in control of his body as his arms move around her to embrace her much shorter body. Carol, on the other hand, is too excited to control herself. She tries to pick him up and nearly does. She's a strong girl.

Nathan looks around the neighborhood and directs his attention down the street. He's expecting someone. Off in the distance, a car is headed in this direction. Nathan waits while he rubs Carol's back, as she's not willing to let go of her brother.

"Is she coming?" Carol looks up to ask him.

He nods. "She should be here any minute."

Fuck.

I'll have to put off my plan until after Penelope leaves.

When the car gets close enough for me to recognize it, I see Penelope driving, and her mother is in the seat next to her. Penelope's hair is down, the way I like it—sweeping to one side, gathering in a large bunch over her shoulder, creating one twist instead of the hundreds they shape on their own when flowing in the back.

The ladies open their car doors, and Carol stands to the side, waving excitedly at Penelope, while Nathan moves to help them get stuff out of the back. Just as he bends down, my anticipation gets the best of me. I want to see what he's helping them with in the back of their car, but my ankle gets caught on a branch running close to the ground. I lose my balance, and since I'm squatting close to the ground, it's hard to recover once my weight shifts too far.

My hand flies back and catches me as best I can. I made a lot of noise while shifting and moving within the bushes, but I still so as not to cause any more damage than I might have already created.

"Carol, why don't you go inside the house and tell Mom they're here?"

Immediately, the pounding of heavy feet clambers up to the front porch.

I hear the sharp tap of footsteps on the cement path that leads between the two homes. I try not to breathe in a way that becomes audible. Short, shallow, calm breaths.

"Nathan, what are you doing?" I hear Penelope call out to him.

His feet shift, only about a yard from where I'm lying, still in an awkward position. "I thought I heard something," he says.

"Maybe it was an animal," Penelope offers.

That's my girl, protecting me.

It takes a few moments, but Nathan eventually gives up on whatever he thought might be happening and returns to help Penelope and her mother to help move a bottle of wine, a casserole dish, and a large shopping bag full of presents out of the back of Penelope's car.

The front door opens again, and Mrs. Barker comes out of the home to greet her guests. "Hello," she says with an elongated O at the end. Her arms open wide for both women, but she devours Penelope with a hug first.

"I'm so happy you could make it," she says to Penelope's mom.

The two moms hug each other as they try and scope each other out for the first time—and, hopefully, the last.

"We're just so thrilled to have been invited. I had the pleasure of spending time with Nathan earlier today." Her hand moves to Mrs. Barker's upper arm. "And you have raised the most wonderful son."

Nathan's mother moves her hands up to the center of her chest. "Thank you," she says, oozing with sincerity. "Now, let's get inside; it's getting cold out." She waves over to her son. "Nathan, grab that bag from Penelope. Don't make her carry it in."

He does as he was told even though his arms are full. Penelope, trying not to laugh at her boyfriend who just got scolded by his mother, drops the shopping bag handles over his outstretched fingers, underneath the casserole dish.

"Yes, Mother," he moans sarcastically but holds an endearing look on his face in her direction.

Once the front door closes behind them, I know I can move without them hearing me disturb the brush around me.

The wind picks up again, and my body shakes from the chills. They're all greeting each other inside, so now is my opportunity to go to my car.

I open the back door and grab a brown blazer I recently bought. I tear off the tag and put it in the pocket along with the latex gloves. I still might need them later—after Penelope leaves the house. This added layer will help me last a few more hours while I watch my girl with the Barkers and wait for them to leave.

When I get back to the residence, I move higher, closer to the neighbor's house where I have a view of the kitchen and dining room table.

It's as if I were watching a movie. The warmth isn't just trapped inside the home; the people within are illuminating it and projecting it upon each other with their smiles, embraces, and laughter.

Mrs. Barker moves about the kitchen, as if every station were an extension of her arm. My mother has never cooked, and I can't recall ever seeing her in our kitchen. My childhood home didn't have the openness that the Barkers' home has. My kitchen was closed off so as to not expose the chef or the help while they worked. What I'm looking at here is complete and utter exposure. They are being vulnerable with each other.

Mr. Barker is loving toward his wife, and she returns his affection. Even when I followed Mr. Barker last week, I didn't find any evidence that he had any extramarital affairs. This must be what a real family looks like—warm, open, and honest with each other with nothing to hide.

The only time I have ever felt vulnerable is when I speak with Michelle. She's the only one I've ever felt compelled to share parts of myself with even if they are very small confessions.

I can't deny my distaste for Nathan. I loathe him and what he's done to me. But, watching all the other people in his parents' home, I can't help but feel the weight of guilt fall inside my belly.

During dinner, Carol finishes her food before the rest of the party and feels the need to leave her seat, so she stands up and goes to my Penelope.

How can she resist the softness of Penelope's skin and the breath that falls around her?

Carol scoots herself up onto Penelope's lap and rests her weight over her body.

Penelope's eyes close, and she breathes in the moment, feeling so much love and happiness in her arms.

A knot balls in my throat. I look down the side of the house and see the black residue from the fire I tried to start. I can't punish this family for Nathan's bad deeds. I can't punish Carol, and I can't punish Penelope.

TWENTY-FOUR

I slept in my car Christmas Eve and watched Penelope and the Barkers open presents the next morning. Nathan gave Penelope a helmet with a pink cursive *P* on the sides. It has the same shape and visor across the face as the spare he has been letting her use. She seemed grateful and happy to receive it, but I felt it was a pointless gesture. She shouldn't be on the back of that crotch rocket anyway. It's dangerous.

The Barkers' friends, the Pendletons, stopped by and had breakfast. They seemed like one big, happy family.

It's what I want for Penelope, but it also creates some kind of anger and resentment in me. If she only knew what I was doing, what I was creating for her. I am creating *her*. She has no idea, yet I feel unappreciated for my efforts.

I force those feelings in the direction of one person—Nathan. The man who, after breakfast, decided to walk around the backyard in the early morning cold, sipping his coffee. He found the pom-poms sitting under the black residue on the side of the house.

I should have moved those last night, knowing there was an identical pair inside, but I got too distracted, watching Penelope enjoy herself within the warmth of the home.

After he picked up the pom-poms and ran his finger over the black siding, he mouthed the words, *What the fuck?*

I'm not sure what conclusion Nathan came to, but I do know I didn't leave any evidence behind that would incriminate me. The latex gloves I'd used remain sitting in my jacket pocket.

When I get into my apartment, I have nothing to do. I left Penelope at Nathan's house. I'd had enough of the Barker family and their happy dwelling. Plus, after sleeping in my car, I feel sore and tired.

Grabbing an orange from my fruit tray on my kitchen island, I peel it before taking the bare fruit and plopping down on my couch, enjoying each bite of the citrus.

I pull out my phone to see I have a text.

> *Michelle: Merry Christmas! I get back to campus on Thursday. I have something for you. Can we meet?*

It's Christmas Day, and this is my joy, my moment of companionship when Michelle reaches out to me. As far as I know, neither of my parents has tried to reach me. Michelle is my only contact with another person. Penelope had hers, and now, I get to experience mine. The anticipation of seeing Michelle this week brings a warmth inside me that I've been envying for the past twenty-four hours.

> *Alex: Merry Christmas. I'd love to see you when you return. You know where I live. I'll be here.*

It's a date, I think to myself and put my phone on the console to my side. I only mean that figuratively. Michelle is just a friend.

Michelle mentioned her flight wouldn't get in until early afternoon, so I know she won't be stopping at my apartment before then.

I lace up my tennis shoes and stand, allowing the hem of my jogging pants to fall over my newly tied laces.

There she is—the figure I've been waiting for—around the bend of the park. I've been tracking Nathan's ex-girlfriend's routine, and this is the most constant. It's finally time for me to make my move and approach her.

I begin jogging at a slow enough pace for her to catch up to me. Once she's at the right distance behind me, I pick it up, as if I were trying to win a race.

I only allow myself a few steps before I purposely become clumsy and trip over my own feet. "Ah!" I yell out loud to ensure I grab her attention. Making sure to stumble enough to kick up dust and seem as if I were having a difficult time getting my bearing, I fall right in the middle of the jogging path and grab my ankle, calling out in pain.

She slows, as I hoped she would, and begins to walk the rest of the way to me. "Are you okay?" she asks, bending down over my injured body.

"Ah, damn it," I say, still holding on to my right ankle. "I think I twisted my ankle. Shit."

She moves her hand, as if she wanted to take a look, but my fingers cover too much surface area. I continue to roll on my back, as if the pain were so great, not giving her a chance to examine my injury.

She kneels down. Her hands move over in frustration in front of her own body. "What can I do?" she asks.

"Well, I can't jog anymore," I tell her, trying to roll onto my side. "Maybe you can help me get to my feet, so I can try and make it to my car."

"Sure." She stands up off her knees and offers her hand out to pull me up.

I make sure to apply just enough pressure for her to understand I'm really struggling with putting weight on my right foot.

"Thanks," I tell her once I'm fully upright. I start to take a step, so I can make it to my car, but I limp so heavily, it would be impossible for me to make it on my own.

As she watches me struggle, her hands wave in front of her again. "Here," she says and grabs my arm, throwing it over her head. "Let me help you."

She aids me as I hop toward the parking lot at the edge of the park. "Thank you so much for helping me. You're being too kind. Can I buy you a cup of coffee?" My chin lifts and points toward the café across the street, on the other side of the parking lot. "I can probably get a bag of ice for my ankle there," I add before she has a chance to turn me down.

Not answering right away, she thinks for a moment. "Well, my run is just about over. I was gonna stop at this point anyway."

I know.

147

She thinks for another moment. I don't dare distract her from contemplating my offer. She's on the tipping point, and I don't want to shove her in the other direction.

"Sure," she eventually says, "I'd love a cup of coffee."

Instead of showing her where my car is, with her help, I hobble along across the lot to the nearby shops.

It's a chain, but I don't care. I have a greater purpose for being here with her than to taste a good and authentic cup of coffee.

Since it's still winter break and even the politicians seem to be spending time at home with their families, there aren't enough people around to form a line inside the coffee shop. I order both our drinks and ask for a bag of ice.

After we sit down and I prop up my leg on a chair next to our table, I try to avoid any moments of silence by asking her a question right away, "So, you go to school around here?"

She nods. "The community college. I'm a junior," she explains.

But I already know all this.

I place the ice-filled plastic bag on my ankle and wince when it touches down, showing how sensitive my foot is and making sure she feels it was necessary to help me out of the park.

"My sister is a junior at Tafford," I lie, looking for a reaction, trying to spark a memory of someone she knows there.

But the girl just smiles and nods.

I shake my head, appearing to think about the imaginary sister I created. "My sister...she has so many horror stories about dating. She just seems to find one jerk after another." I look at her over the rim of my coffee cup. "I bet you've got a few horror stories yourself."

"Oh"—she rolls her eyes—"I've had some terrible blind dates."

I smile and lean back, playing along, as if we were amused with each other. "So, your last relationship, was that from a blind date?"

She pauses before taking a sip of her coffee. "No, actually"— she sets down her drink—"I met him at a party while I was with my friends."

"Do you hate your friends for not saving you from that disaster?"

She moves her tongue around in her mouth, as if she were picking at something. "Why do you think it was a disaster? How do you know I'm not still with him?"

I lean forward to adjust the ice pack on my foot, giving myself time to come up with an adequate answer. "Because I thought we already established it was your last relationship. I think that it is safe to assume it ended." I sit back up and smile, trying to make her feel more comfortable.

She breathes out and rolls her eyes. "Of course." She leans back further in her chair, letting go of more tension.

She's comfortable, and I trust she'll share honest information with me.

"My last relationship wasn't a disaster at all."

Damn. That's not what I wanted to hear.

"If it wasn't a disaster, then why did it end?"

She shrugs and takes another sip of her drink. "He was wonderful actually. Any woman would be lucky to be with him. It ended with us because we knew he was leaving for a year abroad...Italy," she tells me. "I just felt like I was too young for a long-distance relationship. I guess he felt the same because we both seemed happy, breaking up before he left." She sets her cup down on the table. "We stayed friends until he went to Italy, but then at some point over the year, we stopped talking." She shrugs again. "You know, just fizzled out. Great guy but wasn't meant to be."

I tap my index finger on the wood table, creating a burst of sound every time my fingernail drives down and makes contact with the surface. This girl has become useless to me now.

"You know, I forgot there's somewhere I need to be. The ice has made a big difference. My ankle seems fine now." I stand up and ignore the look of skepticism on her face when I place weight on my right foot. "Thanks for your help," I say in a dry tone before walking out the door.

That was no help at all.

"Any woman would be lucky to be with him." Her words come back to me as I walk through the parking lot.

My fist clenches, and I thrust it out, punching the side door of a red sedan on the way to my car. There's no dent, but the action relieved some of the built-up stress I'm feeling.

I'm still angry and racking my brain for another plan to get rid of Nathan as I pace back and forth in my kitchen.

There's a knock at the door. I already alerted the front desk that Michelle would be stopping by, so her name was on the list to proceed up to my apartment.

I open the door, immediately turning my back. "Come in," I say as I walk back to the open kitchen.

I can't seem to get out of this mood I'm in. I want to plan something that will harm Nathan.

"What's wrong?" Michelle asks, still standing in my doorway.

I pause and turn back around. I take a deep breath, calming and cleansing myself, before I speak to her again. "Something was just on my mind. Please, come in," I say again but in a much more welcoming way.

TWENTY-FIVE

Michelle steps in but cautiously moves so as not to miss anything around her, checking out every detail of my apartment with genuine interest. Her eyes and head move in every direction with each step until she looks ahead at the living area. She gives a subtle, slow gasp. "You have a gorgeous view here. Everything about your apartment is beautiful, but the view"—her hand goes out in front of her, palm up, as if handing it to me on display—"it's really nice."

Her comment makes me realize that, other than a cleaning crew, nobody has ever been in my apartment since I moved in. I've never shared this view with anyone before.

It makes me realize there are only two women I ever want to share anything with, and Michelle is one of them. She's becoming very dear to me, and I'm feeling more and more possessive over her.

"Thank you." That gives me pause to look out the windows and enjoy what she's experiencing, but my eyes stop when they get to her.

I observe her figure and profile as she stands to my side. She's wearing the same peacoat I saw her in on campus weeks ago. Her brown hair falls past her shoulders but seems thick and full of life.

I've never noticed it before, but the light is hitting her just the right way. There's one strand around her face that's lighter than the others. The way it blends in tells me it's a natural highlight. It frames her face beautifully.

Her purse, hanging over her left shoulder, makes her tilt just slightly. From the side, I notice how petite her nose is and how her round eyes look like jewels sitting above it. Her cheekbones puff out into balls, squinting her round eyes when she smiles.

"You're right," I tell her. "It is a really nice view."

I look away just as she turns toward me.

"I got you something," she says and moves her purse closer to the front of her body.

She takes one strap off her shoulder and widens the opening of her bag.

I can't understand why women need such large bags on a regular basis. *What more could she need to carry other than her wallet, phone, and keys?* I'm lucky to have all those items fit into my jean pockets. No baggage.

Michelle moves her hand and rummages through until her arm stops. She takes a deep breath before pulling it out. "I hope you don't think it's stupid, but I saw it and thought of you."

I watch carefully as she reveals the gift. It's a glass ball with a bright orange poppy flower trapped inside.

She extends her arm and hands the glass to me. "I saw it in a gift shop at Pike Place Market while I was at home in Seattle. I thought it was pretty, and I remembered what you told me about liking poppies."

I take the ball from her palm and hold it in my fingers near my face to study the flower inside. It's a large poppy with the stem cut off, so it's just the beauty of the petals forced to curve with the edge of the glass. It looks alive and colorful, but it's preserved to stay forever still and bright. The bottom of the ball has a flat surface, so it won't roll away when it's set on a table.

"It's a paperweight," she explains when she sees my thumb rub across the smooth, flat bottom.

I bring my hand down from my face and look at Michelle. "I don't know what to say."

She smiles nervously. "Well, if you like it, you can say, *Thank you*. Or"—she tilts her head to the side—"if you think it's stupid, you can say, *No, thank you*, and give it back to me."

I look down at the glass ball in my hand and then back up to Michelle's caramel-espresso eyes. She seems anxious to hear a response from me.

"No," I begin to speak. Michelle looks increasingly uncomfortable, so I speed up my response. "Nobody"—I take a few deep breaths, my chest feeling very heavy—"has ever thought enough about me to buy me a gift like this." I look down and then back up to her, hoping I can give her gift justice. "Thank you," I say slowly, wanting her to feel and understand the power behind every syllable.

She exhales, relieved by my gratitude, but a sadness falls over her expression. "How could you say that? I'm sure your parents or friends and family have bought you plenty of things."

"My parents..." I say quickly and with too much anger. I swallow and give myself time to correct my tone before continuing, "My parents only have assistants and personal shoppers buy all their gifts. For each other and for me. I didn't have friends growing up, and there's no extended family I have a relationship with."

I lose eye contact and search the room for something else to focus on until I catch Michelle's movements out of the corner of my eye. Her body seems so soft and welcoming at every curve and inch.

"I'm so sorry." She begins to take a step toward me, but I step back behind my kitchen countertop, using it as a shield.

"I don't need your pity," I bark at her and shake my head. "I just need..." I've lost my words.

Her eyes remain patiently focused on me. She's waiting to hear about what I need, but I'm not sure I know.

Penelope?

But she's not here. Only Michelle and her warmth are here.

I look down to what's in my hand. *And this.* Her gift is here.

"This is all I need." I hold it up for her to see.

A smile of satisfaction pulls across her face from cheek to cheek, making her big, round eyes squint from the lack of room. I feel as if my words released weight from her shoulders.

"I'm so glad you like it," she says with relief.

I want to reach out and run my hand over her puffed out cheeks, but I know that wouldn't be appropriate. My heart beats faster, as if I'd been running, but I stopped exercising several hours ago. I wonder if something is wrong with me.

"I need some water. Would you like some?"

She shakes her head, and I turn to pull a glass from my cabinet. While my hand is out to fill my glass with water from the refrigerator dispenser, I notice the clock. It's almost six.

I realize how hungry I am. "Can I buy you dinner tonight?"

"Yes," she answers. Then, her fingers play with themselves in front of her. She takes a step forward and rests her hands on my countertop. "I don't know."

I set down my glass and look at her, confused. Either she's hungry or she's not. I don't understand.

"I thought about you a lot while I was gone, and I wasn't expecting that," she goes on to explain. "But I'm not sure what that means. I've been upset about my breakup with Kevin. You're such good friends with him, and you and I have become good friends—"

I stop her by holding up my hand. "Kevin is not my friend." Just as I say that, my phone vibrates on the countertop. I reach over and pick it up.

Kevin: Where the hell have you been? Club tonight at nine. Be there.

"Kevin?" she asks while my eyes read the text.

Without typing in a reply, I place my phone back down where it was before. "Fuck Kevin. I read once that we are the average of the five people we surround ourselves with. Scientifically, that's bullshit," I add. "But, if by a miracle that's in any way true, he's damaged both our averages."

I wouldn't usually recite such a useless and mundane claim, but I thought there was a chance it could make her smile. I was right.

Her mouth widens, trying not to laugh. "Yeah, fuck Kevin." She steps back and lets her hands slide off my countertop. "Maybe we should talk about *this* later." Her hand moves back and forth between us. "And we can do dinner some other time. I'm still feeling confused about a few things."

I don't understand what she's talking about. I don't understand why she's confused. If she's not hungry, then we won't eat. *What else is there to consider?*

I nod, appearing like I understand. Maybe she will join me for dinner tomorrow when she can better plan for it.

No. Nathan asked Penelope out to a movie, and I want to be there for her as much as possible. I don't like the idea of them having the opportunity to have sex without me being able to interrupt it somehow.

Sunday night, there's a big party at the club for New Year's Eve. Brandy will be back, and I know Penelope will want to go. The girls have gone every year. No doubt Nathan will be tagging along as well. That means, I'll need to go, too. I'll need a date. Michelle seems like the most viable option to use.

"Michelle"—I stop her before she takes another step to leave—"how about New Year's Eve?"

She shakes her head. "I don't have any plans."

"Will you come with me to the club to celebrate? You'll need a dress. People dress up," I tell her, assuming she'll say yes.

I walk with her as she moves toward my front door.

"I have a dress," she says, standing at the front door, turning to face me before leaving.

She looks up to my face as she contemplates an answer. It gives me another opportunity to look into her eyes.

"As far as brown eyes are concerned, I think yours might be the most beautiful."

My words surprise me almost as much as they seem to surprise her. They make me realize my offer to take her to the club on Sunday isn't just about being in the same room as Penelope. I want to be in the same room as Michelle, too.

"Okay," she says, "I'll go with you to the club on New Year's Eve."

That knot in my throat forms again, and my chest feels like it's full of lead. I knew she would say yes, but I can't explain the reaction I have over it.

"It's a date," she says and reaches back to the door handle.

I grab the edge of the door with my hand and pull it open as she steps out. "A date," I breathe as she disappears down the hall.

As soon as the door closes behind me, my hand comes up to my mouth, and I begin biting my fingernails. Small, chipping bites. I'm worried about myself. I move my hand to the side of my neck and use the tips of my fingers to find my large, pulsing vein. When I feel the rhythm of my heartbeat, I press into it harder, testing my pulse.

My hand moves again, to over my chest. It's the same raging heartbeat. I realize what this feeling is. I'm nervous. That's an emotion I shoved away several years ago, as it served me no purpose. But, now, I wonder if it's giving me a warning sign or trying to point me in a certain direction.

TWENTY-SIX

I got an e-mail earlier today that I'd be receiving another award for my research. Sci Gen Labs is creating a prototype for my theories in genetic mapping. They're creating a pod—or, in other words, an artificial womb for me to play with genetic makeup and human creation.

At the time, I felt the weight of my accomplishments. I had the urge to forward the e-mail to Michelle, but then I remembered that one of the things she likes about me is my humility. I thought better of it. I tossed aside my foolish pride and decided to focus on something else.

Right now, I can't think of anything other than Penelope. I decided not to hurt Nathan's family, but that doesn't mean I don't want to hurt him.

He's holding her hand almost a block ahead of me on this dimly lit sidewalk. If I close my eyes, I might imagine it's me she's walking next to. It's me on this date with her.

There are only three shows playing at this small theater. He's taking her to see a romantic comedy.

He purchases their tickets at the outdoor kiosk. I wait outside, pretending to look at the Coming Soon posters. But they are lit up for me to watch them at the concession stand as they order popcorn. The man behind the counter hands Penelope a bottle of water.

Nathan signs the receipt before taking her hand and leading her off toward the theater. That's my cue.

I walk up to the kiosk and purchase my own ticket. The young lady behind the glass booth looks around me after I ask for one ticket. I hope she doesn't find it suspicious that I'm going to a

ERIN LOCKWOOD

movie alone. I look around myself, seeing if there are any other couples so that I can make it seem like I'm part of their group. But nobody else is around. This movie has been out for over a month. People either haven't been interested in seeing it, or they have already had plenty of time to make it to the movies.

Penelope is different. She focuses on academics. She's never cared to go to the theater before.

The lady takes my credit card and swipes it for only the one ticket. I wonder what she's thinking. Maybe I should have asked Michelle to join me.

I walk right past the concession stand. I'm not here for snacks.

Slowly, I open the door to the theater room that's showing the movie Penelope came here to see with her boyfriend.

I look around, hoping not to bump into Penelope or Nathan. I can only assume they've already taken their seats. The darkness in the room is my ally.

I take the left hall down the back of the stadium seating, heading to the far side of the theater. More likely, they have gone to the right side since it was the closest option to them when they opened the door.

When the room opens up, I can spot their moving bodies in the fifth row, close to the right side, as I hoped. I go all the way to the top, the very last row, and find a seat in the middle, below the projector. There are only about eight rows between us, and I can almost feel her hair next to me.

Only one other couple enters the theater before the curtain parts, and the previews begin. Penelope and Nathan are laughing, but once the dim lights turn completely off and the screen illuminates the room, they sit back and quietly watch the show.

I'm not even sure what's going on. I can see the movements and hear the dialogue float in the air around me, but I'm only focused on my girl. I'm watching her watch.

So many times throughout the film, Nathan turns his head and stares at her. Unknowingly, she just keeps watching the film. She laughs, and it's as if the heavens opened. Nathan and I both can't take our eyes off her. For the rest of the movie, he just keeps his head turned to the side, staring at her, as if she were some sort of miracle.

While he's staring and soaking in everything that she is, something distracts him from what he was previously focused on.

Something inspires him to move his head and look around the theater.

He turns his body far enough around that he's looking directly behind them—directly to where I'm sitting—but he squints from the light of the projector. He tries to shade his eyes from the glare, but it's no use because the light is too strong.

I can see you, but you can't see me. Finally, I feel like I have the upper hand again.

I drive carefully, knowing she's on the back of that crotch rocket. Every time I change lanes, I think about the butterfly effect of my actions on the road. *How will the car in front of me react? How will all four of the cars between Penelope and me react to the chain reaction of my car's slight movements?*

A crash on a motorcycle could be deadly.

The fact that she wears that helmet every time she gets on the back of his bike brings me some comfort. But her poor, delicate body wouldn't survive such a brutal attack if she were to collide with another vehicle.

Every maneuver I make is calculated. It always is where she's concerned.

I relax once we're in the residential area near campus. The streets slow to a maximum of twenty-five miles per hour, only blocks away from her apartment. He pulls into the small lot in the back of the building with parking spaces dedicated to the renters. I park a few blocks down, knowing exactly where they're going, and get out to walk closer to the apartment complex.

I walk along the buildings on the opposite side of the street, always careful to hide myself within the shadows cast by the streetlights. I end up settling behind a car, using the untinted windows as my shield while it provides an unobstructed view of my girl.

After they dismount and secure the helmets, he walks by her side along the back of the apartment complex, toward the front of the building. When they get near the mailbox, he stops her by pulling her arm and forcing her to turn toward him.

I hate that fucking mailbox.

"There's something I want you to know before we go up to your room." He swallows hard, gathering courage. His chest is heaving with anticipation of something.

When Penelope looks concerned, he pulls her closer to him, holding her against his chest with his left arm wrapped behind her. She could be imprisoned, but there's no sign of distress on her face. In fact, she looks like she wants to be there.

He brings his right hand up and runs his knuckles down her soft, pale face. Even from a safe distance, I can see her dark-as-midnight navy-blue pools looking up to him. Her lips are swollen, creating her natural pout of succulent pink lips. She looks good enough to taste.

"Penelope, I love your face." He bends down to kiss her blushing cheek. "I love your eyes." He moves to kiss over her lids, and she closes them lightly as he nears. "I love your lips." He doesn't kiss them, but I can see she's anticipating it. He just moves his index finger over the swollen bumps. "I love your heart." He places his hand over her chest. "And, Penelope, I love you. I am madly in love with you. And I'm not sure it's something that can ever possibly go away."

Her slow intake of air inflates her chest and sucks him in. She draws him to her. It's her doing that makes him know he can devour her with his lips.

Son of a bitch!

Their hands begin to curl, as if they were holding something back. They want to dig into each other's skin. Their tongues peek out and swap, wanting so desperately to taste more of each other.

"Nathan," she says, trying to peel herself off him for a moment, "I love you."

A swell builds up in my sinuses. *No. No.* I've never heard her utter those words to another man. *No. No. No.* This is wrong.

Nathan grabs her face on both sides and pushes himself onto her mouth again. The pure power of it makes her step backward a few times, bringing him with her.

Oh God.

They're as desperate for each other as I feel for her. It's like my world as I know it has crashed and become nothing but dust. In only just a few months, Nathan has come in and destroyed everything. Two months ago, she was mine. And, now, this...

I'm overwhelmed with anger and pain coming from my chest.

I watch them walk up to her apartment, hand in hand, and close the door behind them. Knowing they're alone in there, knowing what they're going to do to each other, I look around, wanting something to take away my pain.

I want to rid this feeling out of me. My fists fold and clench with desire to hit something. I don't know what, but I need to hit something. Pulling my arm back, I grunt as I expel anger out of my mouth and set my swing in motion.

Blinding light rises behind me, and I know I'm standing in a spotlight. But it's too late; there's no stopping my arm from moving forward and nothing stopping my fist from hitting the brick building in front of me.

"Ah!" I scream out loud and shake my wrist. "Fuck, that hurt."

"Hold it right there. Don't move." Officer Smith steps out of his black-and-white Ford Crown Victoria with his right hand on his hip and a flashlight in the other. "Why am I not surprised to see you?"

Since my right hand is throbbing, I hold up my left to shield my eyes from the light. "I think the flashlight is a little excessive since you still have your headlights on."

Officer Smith doesn't react to my sarcasm; he stays in place, not moving his hand from his hip. "Why don't you tell me what you're doing here and why you decided to take a swing?" His chin lifts, and he directs his eyesight to the building behind us.

I move my fingers and try to coax the circulation to return, willing my joints and bones to move as they're meant to. I don't think I broke anything, but a thin layer of blood is smeared across my knuckles.

"Would you believe me if I told you he started it?"

I want to laugh at my clever quip, but Officer Smith doesn't seem to think it's funny. Michelle would have liked that line. She would have smiled and laughed through her nose. But I don't think I'll ever be telling her about this incident.

It gives me a thought. *What if this is something I could tell her about? What if I could be open and honest with her about what I did during nights like this?* Something I'd like perhaps, but not something that makes sense. It's too risky.

I straighten up and force myself to look more directly at Officer Smith and the light he's still shining. "Officer, I appreciate you making the rounds, but what I do on the street is none of your business. And, if you have any issues with me and my desire to collect data for research, no matter how minute the material might be, I suggest you take it up with Dean Schumaker."

There. Hopefully, that will be enough for me to be on my way. I've had enough of this horseshit night, and I don't want to waste any more time talking to Officer Smith.

I shake my hand, moving it lower to my side. "Go find some real criminals." My impatient tone is undeniable.

"Look," he says sternly, "I don't know what you think you're trying to pull. I put a call into Schumaker, and he seems to be your biggest fan, which I'm sure you already know. That doesn't make *me* your biggest fan. And, as far as what is and isn't my business, when you're on my streets in Sacramento, *you're* my business."

He rolls his tongue around his teeth on the inside of his mouth, creating a smacking sound once he pulls his tongue off. "I realize I can't arrest you since it seems you've only hurt yourself, but you'd better watch it."

He turns, and the light that was shining on my face leaves, making my vision blurry until my eyes can adjust.

"Go home," he demands with his back to me.

I intend to. There's nothing but pain for me here.

"There's something off about that guy," I hear him mumble to himself as he gets into his car.

I do as he said—not because he told me to, but because I need to get away. I feel as if I were suffocating on the sidewalk outside her window.

As I walk to my car, something builds up inside me. It's not just Officer Smith. It's Nathan. My hatred toward him could mask any discomfort and penetrating insults Officer Smith tried to throw my way.

My whole car shakes when I slam the door closed. My door closing to an astounding shut solidifies that I'm alone and that I can let it all go. I begin to cry.

I hate Nathan. I hate him so much, and I wish he were dead.

TWENTY-SEVEN

I've been in a daze since Friday night. I didn't sleep until I was able to fall asleep on my couch this afternoon. Now, I have to get ready for the New Year's Eve party at the club. Michelle will be here in thirty minutes.

I breathe deeply, and the insides of my stomach feel as if they smoothed out during the breath I took when my mind mentioned her name. *Michelle.* I try it again. There's a calming sensation, but it only goes so far.

Until this moment, I've only thought about one person for the past two days—Nathan. Even the thought of his name makes my stomach feel as if it were burning inside. I hate him. He has taken everything from me. I'm back to being alone now.

When I first saw Penelope three and a half years ago, it was the first time since I was a boy that I felt as if there were substance in this world. She was sitting alone in the library, leaning on one arm as she studied. The light illuminated around her and reflected off her glowing hair, creating a halo effect. It was as if she were my angel, and my purpose was to be there and watch her. I wanted nothing more than to experience the serenity I did at that moment all the time.

That feeling I had when I was near her became my companion. She became my companion.

Now, I'm back to being alone, and it's all *his* fault.

My hand slides through my white dress shirtsleeve. I tilt my head and let my neck crack. Then, I repeat it on the other side, trying to loosen myself up for the evening.

Buttoning down the front of my shirt, I wonder if I look okay. I think a dress shirt should be tucked in, but I'm pairing it with jeans since the campus seems to feign casualness, even on the most celebratory of nights. Untucked is what will look the most appropriate for me to fit in.

My phone vibrates on my bathroom vanity. It could be Michelle. Maybe she's running late. That won't be good. I have plans to drive by Penelope's apartment on our way to the club.

I pick up my phone and turn it over, so I can see the screen.

> *Kevin: I can only assume you've been out of town and busy.*
> *We're going epic at the club tonight. You'll be there, right?*

I flip it back over and set it back down without responding. I haven't seen him or returned any of his texts since Michelle walked out of the club two weeks ago. I've been too occupied to care, and it's probably best if things stay left unsaid since I never even cared about that asshole anyway.

It isn't what I planned, but I have Michelle now. I'll make it work. This setup is much more tolerable. I really meant it when I told her we were both better off without him. And my new growing possessiveness toward her supports that theory.

There is an echoing hollow sound coming through my apartment. It's a knock at my door, alerting me that Michelle is here. My date has arrived.

Lonely taps on my hardwood floor accompany me to the front door, reminding me that I'm alone. There's no purpose if I can't be with Penelope, yet the lonely taps quicken as I near the entrance to my apartment. Now that the moment is imminent, I'm in a hurry to see Michelle.

When I open the door, more light fills the room, and I realize, at this moment, I'm not alone. The true definition of company is standing in my threshold. Even figuratively, I'm not alone when I'm with her. I feel a little ashamed at my previous thoughts toward loneliness. The idea doesn't give this beautiful woman justice.

"I'm sorry. I'm a little early," she says.

I just stand there, holding the door, not moving to the side and giving her space to come in. I remain still, blocking her way, staring at her blankly.

"Alex, what's wrong?" she asks.

What's wrong? I don't know.

She looks down at herself and fidgets, wondering if my reaction is from her outfit. In a way, yes. Starting at her ankles, my eyes move up her lean legs. I've always thought of her as uninspiringly skinny, but she's just proportioned to her slender figure. As my eyes continue to move up, her legs blend into her glimmering chartreuse dress, right in the middle of her thighs. It's the most dazzling color that reminds me of the coolness of winter and the newness of spring. Her waist curves in above her hips, but then her body takes on the most beautiful, round shape where her breasts are.

The short skirt on the dress, matched with the high neckline and long sleeves, gives just enough for me to want more. She's covered and exposed in the most elegant way.

My heart beats faster as I look to her eyes. The caramel complements the green of her chartreuse flawlessly.

She looks sexy. The sight of her makes my groin throb.

"Nothing is wrong. You just look really beautiful."

Air darts out of her nose, and she turns her head, looking away with a wide, tight-lipped smile. Her cheeks swell and darken into a rose color.

My date is here, I remind myself.

"Can I tell you something?" I ask, still in her way, forcing her to loiter in my building hallway.

She nods and gives me the warmth I need to continue.

"I never thought I would feel the urge to share what I'm about to share with anyone at a moment like this. There's just something about you that makes me want to be more honest."

She shakes her head. "I don't understand."

And how could she? I'm not making sense. All I know is that I want to expose myself to her before I let her in.

"This is my first date," I confess. My words came out slowly, and I know she took in every part of that simple sentence. "Ever," I add.

I wonder if she now thinks I'm a virgin. Maybe I should tell her I'm experienced. But then how could I explain that to her in a way she would understand? Maybe she doesn't understand. Maybe it's none of her business. It's just that I might want it to be her business. I've never shared things like that with anyone, and I'm not sure…

"Is that what you wanted when you asked me to go with you tonight?" Her words distract me from my own thoughts. "A date, not just a companion?"

She looks serious as she takes a step forward, bringing our bodies to an uncomfortably close distance. I could stay like this. Or, I could step back and allow her in my apartment. I choose the latter and move out of the way.

Her high heels echo louder than my hard-sole dress shoes. They clack all the way to the wide windows in my living room. Keeping my eyes on her as she moves inside my home, I close the door behind me. I follow her and watch her cross her arms as she looks out onto the view.

"Did that make you uncomfortable? My confession?" I ask her.

She shakes her head, still facing away from me. "No," she says. "There is such a deep mystery about you. I'm dying to know more." She pauses and tilts her head to the other side. "But," she says, now turning to face me, "is this what you want?" Her arms stretch out.

I haven't thought enough about it to come to a conclusion. "I don't know." It's as honest of an answer I can give her. "Is that what you want?" I ask in return.

Of course not. The more I expose myself to her, the less she's going to want anything to do with me. I don't fit in with her, and soon, she'll see that.

Penelope didn't even give me a chance before I was pushed aside. I didn't even have a chance, and I would have changed everything to make sure I was right for her. When I show Michelle who I really am, there won't be a chance in hell that she'll accept me.

She puts her weight mostly on one hip and twists her lips, as if she were thinking. "I don't know. I haven't analyzed how I feel yet."

I smirk unintentionally, not expecting the answer she gave me. "A psychology grad student who hasn't analyzed something yet. Ironic."

My joke makes her laugh, and it's a domino effect, pushing me down with her laughter. I begin laughing, and I realize once again, I'm not alone. I'm connecting with her in a way I've never connected with another human being before.

"You know what?" She slows down her laugh but continues to hold her smile. "Let's just go have fun tonight, and we can talk about all this later."

"Brilliant. I'll just grab my blazer, and we can take my car."

I'm glad I chose my brown blazer; it matches her eyes and complements her dress.

Penelope's apartment isn't exactly on the way to the club—only a four-block detour.

Michelle points ahead. "You know the club is just down this road."

But it's too late. I'm turning onto Dalton Avenue.

"Oh, I must have spaced. Sometimes, I get to campus this way." I know lying to her is wrong and against my instincts where she's concerned. It's just necessary sometimes when it comes to Penelope.

Michelle looks over at me with her brow creased. She looks away, and then I can feel her turning her head again and looking at me with suspicion. *Does she know I lied to her just now?*

Up ahead, I can see my strawberry beauty in a silver dress. She looks stunning. Brandy is there with her, standing outside a small black sedan. The bass player moves his instrument from the front passenger seat to the back. He must be Brandy's date for the evening.

The girls move to put their hands on the car door handles, but the sound of a motorcycle comes from around the corner.

Nathan slowly pulls up. He uses his toes to steady himself on the bike as he moves as close to Penelope as possible. He says something to her through his helmet visor. And, just before we're about to pass, he revs the motor and pulls out in front of us.

In the rearview mirror, I see Brandy and Penelope get in the car with the bass player and his instrument. There's no room for Nathan to have gotten a ride with them.

I watch him maneuver in front of me, hunched over his motorcycle like the cocky asshole he is. But he's exposed, vulnerable, and alone on a very dangerous contraption.

My foot mindlessly presses down, and my car speeds up closer on his tail.

"Alex."

I can hear Michelle's voice echoing in the back of my mind, but it doesn't fully register. I'm too focused.

I press my right foot down harder, and my car purrs with power gripping the road.

"Alex."

The opportunity is presenting itself. If I want Nathan dead, I can kill him with my car right now.

TWENTY-EIGHT

"Alex!" Michelle's scream brings my mind back into the car. "You're too close!" she exclaims and shoves her hand out, gesturing toward Nathan.

She's right. I'm too close, and I can end all of this right now. All it would take is a little more speed and a sideswipe for things to go back the way they were when Penelope belonged to only me.

The power is in my hands, and I wonder if I have the guts to do it. *I feel like I do. But can I kill someone over my obsession?* I've felt the need many times, but now that I'm faced with the opportunity, I wonder, *will my foot move down and apply more pressure on the accelerator? Can I take his precious life for causing me pain?*

I continue driving as I wait to see if my foot receives the message my brain is sending.

"Alex," she says more calmly and places her hand on my thigh.

Her hand is on my thigh. Such an intimate touch. I look down to her hand on my leg, and my heart feels as if it were punching the inside of my chest with each beat.

My hand goes on top of hers, and I feel that she's more than here with me; she's involved with me, touching me in more ways than one. She would be an accessory to my crime, and worse than doing the unthinkable and killing Nathan, *she* would be gone. If things go back to the way they were before, that would mean I wouldn't have Michelle.

My foot eases off the accelerator. I'll manage my pain over Penelope if it means Michelle will stay in my life. I feel as if I'd do anything to keep her, but I wonder if she would want me if she knew all the dark things I'd done, the terrible thoughts I'd had, and all the secrets I'd kept.

"I'm obsessive," I tell her, turning my head to admire her profile, now relaxed, looking ahead at the motorcycle we're falling further behind. "I think you should know that."

She turns to look at me and leans back against her seat, even more relaxed now. "I know." Her voice is so calm and soothing.

Maybe she doesn't understand.

Her hand begins to move from my thigh, but I grip it tighter, keeping it in place.

"Doesn't that bother you?"

Her other hand reaches across her body, and she softly lays it on top of mine, trapping my fingers between hers. "Alex, I told you, our worst qualities are also our best. There's a good reason for all of our habits."

Habit? My obsession, my Penelope, is more than a habit. Maybe Michelle can understand this over time.

I pull into the parking lot, and even though there are several spots closer to the front doors of the club, I park toward the back. Michelle doesn't ask why.

"Kevin will be here tonight," I warn her while we walk past the other parked cars on our way to the entrance.

She holds a small clutch in front of her and scrunches her shoulders together, so her arms are covering as much of her front as possible. I watch her shoulders shudder in small, rapid spurts. I breathe in, deep and slow, and hope I'm not going to make her uncomfortable by putting my arm around her. Bringing her closer to my body will help keep her a little warmer while we're outside.

I rub my hand along her arm, and the shudders stop. She looks up to me and smiles, thanking me for the warmth.

"I figured," she says. "I'll just avoid him if I can."

Her head moves down and stays low, looking at each step in front of her. I wonder if she's trying to hide the hurt on her face at the mention of Kevin.

Guilt runs through my mind, making me feel tense. I hate that I had any part in her pain by helping Kevin keep his secret for so long. I wish I could shield her from ever feeling pain again. It was all because of my obsessiveness—the *habit* she thinks she can accept.

Her chartreuse dress still shimmers when we're in the dark lighting of the club. When she moves, it creates a disco-ball effect, grabbing any light it can find in the room and reflecting it to share with everyone. The color and vibrancy of the dress is almost as loud as the music.

Before choosing a side to collect a drink, I scan the room, looking for Kevin. Michelle's eyes and head are moving around, too. She must be looking for him as well, but I don't see him.

"I think we're safe."

She breathes out of her nose and looks at me. "It's fine."

She smiles and steps further into the belly of the club. I tap her arm, prompting her to follow me to the bar on the right.

"You don't have to do that," I say once we make it to the side where it's a little quieter.

The bar has an awning over it that seems to shield some of the sound. An obvious design feature for the club's benefit, so the bartender can actually hear drink orders.

She takes a seat on the one empty stool, and I stand beside her.

"Do what?" she asks.

"Pretend like Kevin didn't hurt you."

Her eyes become large, as if she were surprised. "I'm not pretending. He did hurt me," she states clearly. "It doesn't mean I can't smile though."

Then, she does something that completely throws me off. She widens her smile, shows me most of her brilliantly white teeth, and shakes her head, beaming, throwing her smile in my face. I've never seen anything so adorable before.

"Drinks?" the impatient bartender asks.

Michelle swings her legs toward the center of the bar and calls out her order, "Gin and tonic, please."

"I'll have the same." I hand him my credit card to keep on file. "All of her drinks will be on my card."

"Well, thank you," she says. "For a beginner, you're not bad at this date thing."

I want to laugh, but the reminder of my inexperience in interacting socially with people makes me feel insecure. I calculate how to behave, but it's not natural. Not like the way Michelle interacts with people.

"I'm sorry Kevin hurt you." I bring us back to our previous conversation, wanting to focus more on her than my shortcomings. "I'm sorry I didn't stop him or tell you sooner."

"It's okay—" she begins to say.

I quickly interrupt, "It's not okay!" My voice is louder than intended.

Placing her hand on my blazer, where my elbow is, she continues her thought, "Alex, it's okay." She nods her head, and our drinks are placed behind her on the bar. "Pain is necessary to grow. It helps shape who we are."

Pain is necessary to grow? I think about the pain I've been experiencing over Penelope. I go further and think about the pain I experienced long ago when I learned about my parents' phony union. *How the hell did I grow from that shit?*

I was a child with no friends—only my mother and the love I thought she had for me. But she loved enabling my father more than she wanted to give me a home. Her enabling drove her into the arms of another companion. My parents are no different from Kevin. They're both sleeping with other women. My mother has never confided in me, but I know she and Bethany have a physical relationship.

I shake my head, disagreeing with Michelle. "You can't tell me that, if you were offered a guarantee to never feel pain in life, you wouldn't take it."

I lean over her and grab both glasses. She takes the cold glass in both hands.

"No," she says excitedly, "I wouldn't."

As she continues to explain herself, my head is forced to turn. Her words trail off when she notices my attention has moved elsewhere.

I'm not sure if it's habit or will, but I have to look at *her* when she enters a room. The four of them walk in together, but she's the only one I care to see. Nathan's presence only reminds me that I let him live. That was my choice and my gift to him.

You're welcome.

But, as I see Penelope with a smile as bright as the sun, hair moving as if it had its own beautiful personality, and a body that carries itself higher than anyone else in the room, I realize I didn't give her any of the happiness she's been wearing lately. She is taking on a new life without me.

When she moves her fingers after his hand brushes hers and they interlock, I recognize that I gave her that same gift I feel I gave Nathan.

Pain—that's what I would have given her. That's what I saved her from when I didn't follow through with harming Nathan. If I don't feel that Michelle deserves pain, how could I wish that same feeling onto Penelope?

Out of the corner of my eye, I see Michelle's hand reach up. It makes its way to my chin, and she pulls it toward her until I'm staring straight into her eyes. She's forcing me to look at her.

"I wish I could read your mind," she says.

I shake my head, ashamed that I ever looked away from that caramel-espresso color.

"No, you don't."

I'm so torn between these two women—one real, the other…not mine. Not anymore.

"Tequila," the familiar sound of that piece-of-shit asshole calls to the bartender.

Michelle's face contorts into disgust when she looks over my shoulder.

I hear him gasp behind me when he sees Michelle sitting at the bar.

"Michelle," he breathes. "You got my message. You came."

She looks away, as if it hurt to move her eyes. "I'm here," she says as she begins to stand. "But I didn't come to see you, and I'd rather not see you for the rest of the night."

Taking her clutch in one hand and shoving it under her armpit, she grabs on to my arm with the other and lets her fingers slide down until we're holding hands.

"Alex?" I hear Kevin say in confusion as I let Michelle lead me away from the bar.

The crowded club forces people to close around us, and Kevin melts away, as if he weren't even here.

Still holding on to my hand, she takes me to the center of the club and down the five steps toward the dance floor. She turns around and takes two steps backward, just enough to face me. "Let's dance."

My hand comes free from her, and I let it go limp by my side as I come to a halt. "No." I shake my head. "I don't dance. I'll just watch." *I'm good at watching.*

She turns back and reaches down for my hand again. "Look, it's New Year's Eve. Let it be the last thing you do before this year is over. Try something new. It'll be a great send-off."

When I don't budge, she becomes a little irritated and tries a different approach. "Okay, so don't dance, but come with me and stand there while I dance."

Reluctantly, I begin to move with her to the floor. It's so crowded. I could likely just stand there, and enough people would bump into me, moving me, making it appear as if I were dancing. I wouldn't be a very good date if I didn't try. At the very least, I'd like to try for Michelle.

TWENTY-NINE

I'm right about the crowd. There's hardly enough room for anyone to move, but people seem to manage by swaying their weight and bumping next to each other. Oddly enough, it doesn't seem to bother anyone.

To my benefit, there are too many people for Penelope and Nathan to notice how close I am. Even the moments I look only at Michelle, I could smell vanilla and violets in the air.

At one point, I think Penelope's hair might have brushed against me. But there was no way to know for sure since I didn't turn to be certain it was her.

We dance for several songs.

"How much longer until midnight?" Michelle screams over the blaring music. She's braver and louder after her second cocktail.

I reach into my back pocket for the clock on my phone. The first thing that shows on my screen is a message from Kevin.

Kevin: Why the fuck are you here with her?

"Just over an hour," I inform her, swiping the text away.

She gets excited, anticipating the impending countdown. It gives her more energy, and she jumps in the air with her arms up, twisting and turning her body. She's completely offbeat, but her smile is enough for me to join in on the fun. I become braver and move around in a more carefree way.

The heat builds around my body, and my clothes act as an oven. "It's too hot," I tell her and then peel my brown blazer off my shoulders. I find a chair off to the side of the dance floor for me to drape my jacket over.

As my arm moves to lay it over the back of the chair, my eyes catch the daggers directed at me. Kevin is up at the bar, leaning back with his arms crossed in front of him. He's staring down at me, warning me with his eyes.

I really don't give a fuck about you, I warn back. *You'd better stay the hell away from Michelle.*

"Forget about that asshole," Michelle says in my ear behind me. She catches my hand, low at my waist, and pulls me back to dancing with her.

Time goes by as we move and have fun. I feel like I belong here with Michelle.

Between songs, the volume lowers, and an announcement is made. "Twenty minutes until midnight."

The entire club erupts in cheers, and Michelle is no exception. Her arms go up, her fingers wiggle, and she screams, blending into the noise of the room. Her joy is infectious. I can't help but stand back and admire her.

After the quick celebration, the mood in the club changes with the melodic tone of a song coming on. About a quarter of the dancers leave the floor, and only couples remain. There's more space, and I'm feeling exposed.

Before I can turn and bolt off the floor, Michelle raises her arms and places her hands around my neck. She sways, and I sway with her.

She's so close. I can see how the caramel melts into the coffee, like a sunburst illuminating out of the depths of her pupils. I can feel the adoration she has for me in the whimsical way that she's smiling.

I want to hold her even closer, so I press her tighter against my body, feeling the roundness of her breasts and the hardness of her nipples under her dress. We're so tight against each other that her sequins snag on my shirt with every tiny movement.

Her hair moves under my nose, and I can smell her shampoo. My head turns into her neck, and I have this terrible urge to press my nose to it. But then my perspective on the room changes, and strawberry-blonde comes into view.

Penelope is draped over Nathan in a similar way Michelle is pressed against me. I watch them. I watch her move, knowing I know everything about her. We're in the same room, only feet apart, but she's so far away, and I know I'm a stranger to her.

"You like her," Michelle says softly in my ear.

My head pulls back, and I realize she knows I've been staring at Penelope again. "She's my obsession," I admit to more of my dark secret, as if I were asking her about the weather over morning coffee.

Michelle nods, absorbing my admission. She goes back to dancing with her hand on my shoulder, resting her chin over her hand. "I know," she says quietly.

I swallow hard and muse over her acknowledgment of my habit. "How do you know?"

"I've seen you watch her. On campus and"—she pulls back a little and slightly gestures in Penelope's direction—"around. On our way here, I know you didn't space. You drove by her on purpose."

How could she know so much and still be here with me?

I'm exposed, yet I feel as if this were a safe place. If there is something wrong with me for my obsession, there must be something wrong with Michelle to allow herself to be so close to me.

"What's your best quality?" I ask, knowing I'm looking for her theory on the mirror effect of our attributes.

Right on point, she says, "You mean, my worst?"

I smile and quietly laugh through my nose in a similar way she often does. "Exactly."

"I like to fix people," she answers.

You didn't fix Kevin. Is that what she was trying to do?

My foot steps the wrong way, and my toes fall over Michelle's, covering the front of her black high heel. "Sorry." I feel all wrong for her.

She ignores my wrong step and my apology. "I like to fix people," she says again.

That's a beautiful thing for someone to say. It's more complicated and deeper than an answer like, *I work too much*, so that's a good and bad quality simultaneously. Only a boring person would have a boring answer. It only shows how emotionally intelligent she is.

"Explain to me how that can be a poor quality."

I feel her inflate her chest against me as she breathes in.

"Not everyone wants to be fixed." Her monotone voice tells me it's something that bothers her and eats away at her. It might be a flaw in her eyes, but the real flaw belongs to the people she surrounds herself with.

We both lean back to look at each other at the same time. Our bodies, still pressed together, force our gaze to be only inches away.

"That's not your burden to bear."

A stone but warm face is staring into me.

Is she trying to tell me something? If so, I can't read her expression.

I see it; she gives up on me.

Turning her head, she says, "It's getting close to midnight. Should we get a drink?"

She floats off the floor, away from my arms, and my body feels cold in her absence.

I catch her arm before she gets too far. "Please, allow me. I'll go get drinks and meet you back here."

Silently, she agrees, and I stride up the steps to the bar where my credit card is being held.

Kevin is still there in the same position I saw him in not long ago. He eyes me as I near, but I ignore his expression. He doesn't move as I get close to the bar, so I assume he's just there to sulk. *Go right ahead.*

"Champagne…two!" I yell out.

The bartender is buzzing around, moving so fast, sloppily making drink after drink. He looks my way and moves his chin, letting me know he heard my order. He doesn't speak as he works so fast, not wanting to break his concentration.

I lean against the bar with my back to Kevin, so I don't have to endure his sour facial expression. But that might have been a mistake because, just across the bar, Nathan is leaning over, his eyes narrowing in on me.

He moves without losing focus on my face. I can't turn away from him, as it would be too obvious.

He sets down his drinks as he comes to stand next to me. "Do I know you?" he asks, studying my face.

His dark brows furrow as he tries to study even harder now that he's so close.

"Nope," I simply say and look ahead, silently pleading for the bartender to hurry the fuck up.

He shifts his stance and casually points a finger at me. "No, I feel like I've seen you before."

"Not that I can recall," I say with the same expression.

Nathan doesn't give up, and he doesn't stop looking directly at me.

Finally, I've had enough of being a specimen for him to examine. "Look, buddy," I say, ready to tell him to fuck off if he doesn't stop staring at me.

"Were you following me earlier tonight?"

His interruption stops me mid sentence, and I wonder if I'm now expressionless.

Can I argue this? He must have turned his head to get a look while I was driving so closely behind him. He had to have seen me. It's not something I can deny. I'm not entirely convinced that I would have gone through with it, especially with Michelle in the car, but I still feel as if I spared him...yet he's offended.

"A little fast, don't you think? What the hell were you doing? You could have killed me." He ends his statement with a gasp.

Exactly.

Luckily, I'm great at coming up with feasible lies on the spot. "I was a little distracted. My girlfriend was helping me celebrate the New Year a little early." I move my head in an awkward way and move my hand up and down in front of my crotch, so he gets the point.

He nods, as if he believed me, but he still looks upset. "Just be a lot more careful next time." His tone is a little calmer after my explanation.

My drinks finally arrive, and I reach over to take them from the bartender's hands.

"Will do," I say to Nathan as I turn and remove myself from this undesirable situation.

He doesn't protest my departure, but he keeps his eye on me as I descend to the dance floor.

I find Michelle, handing her glass to her as soon as I walk up. "Bubbles for the New Year," I tell her.

"Thank you."

"Less than one minute until midnight." The announcement comes over the loudspeakers. The music turns up, and excitement builds as the impending countdown nears.

Michelle perks up with the atmosphere. My mood perks up, too, as I have the opportunity to admire her in this jovial state.

So beautiful and effortlessly at ease. I watch her chartreuse dress dazzle under the turning strobe light.

She's breathtaking tonight. If I had to choose one moment to freeze time, I'd choose this one. Not just because I get to admire her in front of me, but also because I get to admire her while she's here *with* me. I get to experience the touch, not just the beautiful sight.

As content as I feel at this moment, she makes me feel ashamed of so many things, including ever thinking she was plain. There's nothing simple, plain, or basic about her. My gut tells me, she's more like me than I realize.

She spins, and when her body comes back to face mine, she smiles at me. With her lips still pressed together and stretching out wide across her face, I stare directly at them.

A realization hits me. *I want to kiss her.*

The music stops, and a new voice booms overhead. "Ten...nine...eight..."

THIRTY

"Happy New Year!" everyone shouts at the top of their lungs, confetti fluttering in the air from every direction.

Michelle bounces up and down while I keep my feet planted on the ground. She screams and shouts, celebrating with the rest of the crowd, and I remain silent but happy.

When she comes down from her high, she instinctively turns toward me.

Michelle came with *me*. This is my moment.

She takes a step toward me, and I don't stop her. The noisy room feels quiet in my head as she moves only an inch away from my face.

I don't know how to do this. I've kissed Desiree several times, but that was her job. I was in control, and now…I'm not. This is different. I'm not sure if I hold the skills to be with another person in an intimate way.

Without me having to decide what to do or how to do it, she presses her lips on mine. She holds them there for nearly two seconds before parting.

"Happy New Year," she says.

All I can do is nod, stunned by her gift. *A New Year's kiss.* If I never get anything else again, I'll be happy with having that experience of her lips on mine even if it was just for a short moment.

We continue to dance until the club seems to thin out. I want to let Michelle enjoy herself as long as possible. Plus, Penelope is still here. She's still dancing with Nathan. Brandy and the bass player have already left.

"Wanna call it a night?" Michelle asks, likely observing my trancelike state.

I am tired, but I always seem tired.

"Only when you are," I tell her.

"It's late. I think it's time to go home."

I look over to where Penelope is and feel anxious to leave before her. I've always made sure she got home okay.

Michelle's soft fingers touch my chin for the second time this evening, and she turns my head to face hers. "I think it's time for us to go," she says in the most soothing tone. It's almost like magic that makes me want to float out the door with her.

I nod and do just that as we head toward the exit together.

The night has gotten much cooler. Even during a mild winter, the late California breeze makes the evenings very chilly.

Michelle shudders at the sudden wind and change in temperature. I wrap my arm around her, and she eases.

"This is why you broke up with me? This is why you won't return my calls or texts?"

Kevin is smoking a cigarette behind us. His wrist snaps, and he flings the cigarette to the asphalt.

I'd love to watch this asshat embarrass himself, but he's not worth ruining a great evening.

"You don't need to deal with him. We can just go," I tell Michelle and tug at her arm, just enough to give her the hint.

"What the fuck, Michelle? What the hell are you doing here with him?" he sneers.

Michelle is about to walk away with me, but she quickly turns on her heels and tosses a finger in Kevin's direction. "You can go to hell."

Attagirl.

"How dare you question who I spend my time with after I saw you go off to screw some girl."

Kevin freezes, like he just got shot with a stun gun, knowing he got caught with his hand in the cookie jar.

"Oh, and I'm sure she wasn't the only one." Michelle dramatically rolls her eyes.

He can't defend himself, not reasonably. Especially since I'm here, and I won't be corroborating any of his asinine stories.

His upper body slumps in a submissive sort of way. "Michelle, I'm so sorry," he concedes and feigns remorse.

I've seen this look on several groveling past prospects for Penelope after I exposed them for who they were.

"Fuck off, Kevin," I throw my words at him like I want to throw my fist in his face.

But that makes Kevin perk up and continue to show his asshole colors. "You stay the fuck out of this, Alex," he retorts. "This is between me and Michelle."

I want to possess her. Her business feels like my business.

I think about taking a step toward him to confront him much closer, but Michelle immediately puts her hand on my chest, likely reading my mind.

"No." She whips her head at Kevin. "He's right. Fuck off."

She grabs my elbow and tries to get me to turn around, but Kevin opens his mouth.

"You are a fucking weirdo," he spits in my direction.

He hasn't said anything I didn't already know. I've always felt like a freak. The only thing that makes me feel as if I belong around other people is knowing how needed my intelligence is. But every interaction I've ever had has been a result of my intelligence. Every move I make is analyzed heavily before I make it. Nothing comes easily for me.

"And you," Kevin continues but averts his attention toward Michelle, "are a lousy lay. You guys can have each other."

I've felt like an outsider my whole life. Nothing he says to me could be worse than what I've already told myself. I wouldn't be a good date if I let him talk to Michelle that way. She doesn't deserve this.

I'm gonna fucking kill him.

She can't stop me this time. I dart toward Kevin, my arm flying.

I've dreamed of punching someone every time an unworthy man looked at Penelope, but I haven't actually done it, so I have no clue what I'm doing.

My arm flies, but there's no contact. Kevin steps out of the way and shoves both hands on my back, thrusting me forward, slamming me against the outside wall of the club.

I can taste the cement in the cinder block when my face meets the unforgiving surface. My right cheekbone took most of the impact until my body caught up and my chest slammed into the wall. It felt like such a blow.

"Alex!" Michelle screams and runs to me.

I must look so weak to her.

"Fucking loser," I hear Kevin mutter as he walks off.

I'm consumed with so much shame from the inability to defend my date. I can fix this and inflict revenge later, but right now, I want to be invisible.

She places her hand on the back of my head. "Here, let me see," she asks, trying to force me to move my head and show her my wound.

"No," I snap. "Don't look at me."

"I want to help," she tells me, still pulling at my face.

Her hands are so soothing, and her voice is warm. I give in, and I let her see me.

"Oh," she slowly and softly says.

Her finger grazes the gash I know is on my face. I can feel my blood rushing to my cheekbone. It throbs, and I wish I could look away from her again. Her finger moves too close, and I flinch.

"Are you okay?"

My lip quivers as I sit here, on the ground, making my date bend down over me. Once again, I feel the need to confess my shortcomings to Michelle. "I'm such a loser. I'm so weak." My lip and chin tremble to the point of me wanting to let it all go. I turn my face away from her again and let myself cry as subtly as possible.

"Hey." She sits up straighter, her knees still bent to meet me near the ground. "I can fight my own battles. But, Alex..." Her voice is soft and sincere. She runs her hand across my back and uses the other to bring me out of my shell. I sit up straighter and give her the eye contact she's trying to force. "With that said, that was the bravest thing anyone has ever done for me."

I stand up, bringing her with me, and brush the dirt off the front of my clothes. "I made a fool out of myself!" I yell at her.

"Not to me!" she screams back. "Or do you not care about what I think because I'm not that other girl?" Her hand shoves out toward the club.

"Of course not," I spit out. Then, I allow my heaving chest to slow down. "You make me feel like I could belong with someone. I just...I wanted to be good for you tonight. I wanted it to be perfect for you, but I've fucked it all up."

"Alex," she says, stepping forward and bringing herself close to me, "you do belong, and you have made this night perfect for me."

She leans in cautiously, but then I feel the delicate flesh of her lips pressed on mine again. Instinctually, my hand comes around, and I cup the back of her head, allowing her hair to fill my fingers. I kiss her back, and a knot forms in my throat as my heart beats faster.

I release her mouth from mine and lean back enough to see her beautiful face. "Was that kiss real?" I ask. She looks confused, so I explain further, "Was it real, or was it because you felt obligated, like the celebratory kiss you gave me?"

She shakes her head. "Oh, Alex. How could someone so smart be so stupid?" She makes a playful tsking sound with her mouth. "I would never kiss anyone for any other reason than because I'd chosen to. I wanted to kiss you because you had made this night so perfect. I don't need someone who's stronger than other men; I want someone who cares about me more than other men."

"Everyone wants to feel special."

"And there's nothing wrong with that."

I run my palm over her cheek, moving my fingers into her hair and brushing it away from her face. "You are very special to me."

THIRTY-ONE

All the excitement created some adrenaline in us both, but the recent gust of wind that whirls by us makes Michelle shiver. Her arms wrap around her body, coaxing more warmth.

"Can we talk about this more at my apartment? Where it's warm."

She nods, her hands still crossed over her front. "We should probably get some ice on that." She winces, looking at my cheek. "Are you okay to drive, or should we call Student DD? They have extra cars on call tonight."

"I'm fine to drive," I assure her and then begin to look around, realizing I don't have my blazer. "I left my jacket inside."

She stops walking and places her delicate hand on my arm. "I can go get it for you."

"Please. You'll be warm inside, and I'll pull the car around to the front. It's to the left of the dance floor, over a chair."

"Okay." She smiles and then breaks off toward the entrance.

I wait and watch her as she moves away from me. I feel ashamed that I'm not capable of protecting her physically, but I still feel the need to watch her and make sure she gets inside without any incident. There's something inside me that tells me I'm stronger than I really am.

She makes the short walk to the entrance and then passes through. Just as the door closes behind her, it stops before shutting. Nathan pushes it back open and allows Penelope to move past him.

I've been still, watching Michelle, but now, I'm remaining still, watching Penelope move out of the building.

"Are you sure you remembered my new helmet?" I hear her ask Nathan.

"Yes, baby. We're all set." But when he lifts his head once they're both through the door, he spots me under the parking-lot lighting, placing me under a spotlight for him.

Nathan's expression changes, and he takes Penelope's hand and steps to the side of her, shielding her from me.

He doesn't need to protect her from me. *Does he think I would ever hurt her?* I've done nothing but protect her since the moment I first saw her beautiful face and mesmerizing hair.

"Baby, you know what? I think we should actually take a cab," he tells her, trying to move her to the side, further from me.

I feel my brows crease. I should be happy that she's not going to ride on something so dangerous, but I resent the reasoning. He's worried about me hurting her if she rides on the motorcycle with him.

"Why?" she asks, confused.

"It's just better if we take a cab." He pulls his cell phone out of his back pocket.

"But..." Penelope is still confused. "You only had one drink, and that was hours ago. We don't live far, and I know you don't want to leave your bike here overnight," she tries to argue with him.

But his concerned expression doesn't budge.

He takes his eyes off his phone for a moment and looks directly into her navy pools. "I don't care about the bike as much as I care about making sure you get home safely. Can you just trust me?"

She nods and doesn't argue with him anymore. Keeping her close, Nathan goes back to dialing a phone number.

He is trying to protect her from me?

"I would never hurt her!" I scream out to him.

He takes Penelope's arm and moves her a little more behind him. "Look, buddy," he shouts back, "I don't know what your problem is, but you need to stay away."

Stay away? I don't think I can do that.

"Penelope," I beg for her understanding, "I would never hurt you. Never."

We're maybe a hundred feet away. I can see she wants to step forward to get a better look at me, but Nathan is blocking the way, so she just tries to study me from afar.

"I'm sorry. Do I know you?" she asks.

I swallow hard, wishing I could explain everything to her so that she would know that I would never do anything to hurt her. "No," I finally admit.

She tilts her head and gets a good view of the cut on my cheek. "Are you all right?" she asks and begins to take a step toward me.

Nathan takes her by the shoulders and looks intensely into her eyes. "I saw him on campus, I thought I saw him at the movies, and he was the one following me on my bike earlier tonight. I have a really bad feeling about him. I think we need to keep our distance."

"No!" I yell and shake my head. "It's not like that."

I begin to move closer to her, but Nathan yells at me to stay back.

"Alex!" Michelle calls from the front doors.

She's wearing my jacket, and I wonder how long she's been standing there.

She walks over to me and speaks low so that nobody else can hear her, "Just leave them alone."

I shake my head. "But she doesn't understand."

"*I* understand," she says, raising her voice slightly. "And I'm telling you to just let it go."

I bite my lower lip and fight the urge to bite on my nails. Michelle is probably right. I'm not thinking clearly today.

"Fine," I say. "Come on."

I gesture for us to move to my car, but Michelle doesn't go anywhere.

She looks down and breathes out. "Alex, it's been a really great night, but I think I should get a cab and go home." She can't hide this new disappointment on her face.

I look over and see that Nathan is on his phone, likely calling a cab himself.

"I'll just drive you." The anxiety builds in my chest. *How could everything pick up so much and fall apart so quickly in one night?*

Michelle sheepishly shakes her head. "I think I need a little space to think."

Before I can argue, she's holding her phone to her ear.

I wait patiently until she's done with her call. When she brings it down from her face and places it back in her clutch, she cautiously looks at me.

"I'm confused," I tell her. "Why are you running from me? Why are you taking you away from me?"

In her usual calm tone, she says, "Because I'm confused, too." She shakes her head and lets her hair fall more naturally behind her. "And I'm not running away from you. I just need a little space to think. It's been an incredible night, and I've really had a good time."

"But?" I prompt her to explain more.

"But I'm confused," she continues. "Sometimes, I think we have these incredible moments, and I feel like we're really clicking. Then, the next minute, you can't stop staring at another woman. Part of me wants to love that part of you, but the other part doesn't think it's a good idea for me to get involved with another man who doesn't stare at only me." She moves her small hand up to her chest, comforting herself.

I want to argue with her. I want to tell her that I'll never look in Penelope's way again, but I know I can't make her a promise I won't keep. Even as we stand here, I'm still finding my strawberry beauty in the corner of my eye.

The silence was enough for Michelle. "Okay then." She begins to shrug my blazer off her shoulders.

"No"—I stop her from letting it fall—"take it with you."

I don't wait for her response. I just turn and head for my car.

When the driver door slams, I feel suffocated by the solitude. For a moment, I had it. It wasn't Penelope, but I had a woman in my arms. There were times tonight where I wasn't worried about where my hands were and what angle my arms were resting, so I could fit in. I was just touching her and holding her.

And she kissed me, out of her own free will. It was natural, and I've never encountered anything like it before.

I look across the rows of parking spaces, and my eyes find Michelle. She's just standing there in my jacket and that gorgeous dress, her legs long and lean. She looks as lonely as I feel, waiting for her ride.

Across the stretch of the front of the building stands Penelope and Nathan. She's leaning into him, and he's holding her, his leather jacket draped over her back. Every now and then, his eyes move, and I know he sees me sitting in my car.

I can't move myself from this parking lot until I know she's okay.

Two Priuses, each one with a student DD decal on the side, pull into the driveway. I press the button to turn my engine on. It's almost time for me to leave.

Penelope and Nathan duck down to get into the car. Michelle does the same only seconds later.

Both cars make a loop around the lot, so they can exit. The Prius carrying Penelope and Nathan makes a right turn once the traffic is clear. The second car waits for the right moment but then pulls onto the road, making a wide left turn.

I'm not far behind, but I stop. I look both ways down the busy avenue. First, I look left and then right. Then, I decide to put my left turn signal on. I have to make sure she makes it home okay.

I follow the Prius down streets I've never ventured before, but I make sure to stay far enough behind that she doesn't see me. The dark night sky mixed with my headlights behind her will help ensure that happens.

One block back from where the driver drops her off, I watch the dazzling chartreuse dress exit the car. She says something to the driver while the door is still open, and then she closes it. I wonder what she said to him.

She flips her head, forcing her hair away from her face, and the streetlight catches the shine of the one highlight in her hair that frames her face. I wish I could have pushed her hair out of the way for her.

I stay put and watch her walk into her apartment, and I don't leave until the door is shut behind her. One light turns on, and then the next window illuminates, telling me where her bedroom is. She lives alone. Of course she does.

Everywhere I look, I see Michelle—standing at my kitchen counter, looking out the windows. I remember how in awe she was of the view. I remember her standing in my apartment with her arms crossed, looking out over the campus and the small glimpse of the Capitol.

I've hardly slept more than ten hours in the past three days. Everything is throwing me off—the new semester with new schedules, the absence of Penelope, whom I haven't seen since Sunday night...and the absence of Michelle. I've seen her, but I haven't been near enough to her.

Now that I've experienced it, I need it, and being away from her creates a pain that I can't blame on anyone other than myself.

I'm back where I used to be, following and watching but never touching. Only it's Michelle and not Penelope whom I've been keeping my eye on. Sometimes, I think about approaching her and apologizing to her. But then I realize, she turned her back on me that night. I lost the physical connection I hadn't realized I needed so badly. I'm feeling too insecure to ask for it back now.

I grab my briefcase from the counter and head to my office at the library.

THIRTY-TWO

As I walk the hall, I look over at the study tables, not knowing if Penelope will be there. She has a different class schedule, and I haven't bothered to gather that information.

I've never seen Michelle in the library. I've only seen her walking across campus and at the student center, but I know she's at a lecture right now.

If she saw me here, would she approach me or act as if she didn't know the freak who was pushed into a wall on New Year's Eve? And then later made a bigger fool of himself by yelling at a woman who only knew him as a stranger.

What a fool, I tell myself as I enter my office and close the door behind me.

When I set my briefcase onto my desk, there's a noticeable thud that catches my attention. I open the top and am immediately reminded of the gift Michelle gave me.

My hand covers the glass ball, and I pull it out. *What a glorious poppy,* I think before setting it in the center of my desk.

When I take a seat and slump down, the glass ball is at eye-level. I stare at the flower and its liveliness as I contemplate how something so vibrant and alive could be trapped in a glass bubble. Its only purpose is to be admired and discussed while its destiny is to stay still and trapped.

There's more meaning to this gift. I wonder if Michelle understands me more than I realized. *Could she possibly have the same twisted desires as me?*

Pound. Pound. Pound.

There's a knock at the door, followed by a deep voice. "Alexander George Bishop."

The throaty deep voice almost sounds familiar, but it's hard to fully analyze the throttle on the other side of the door.

In a controlled movement, I pull open the door, not giving in to the urgency this person is trying to expel on me.

"You might be the last person I expected to see here," I tell him, surprised to see him outside my office.

"Yet I'm very happy to see you," Officer Smith says. "Looks as if that wall decided to hit back."

He eyes my cheek, and there's a hint of satisfaction on his face, as if he would have loved to be the one who hit me. I reach up and touch it, feeling for how bad it might look. The swelling has gone down significantly, but it's bruised around where my skin split.

"My gut was right about you," he goes on. "You need to come with me down to the station. It's about time you answer to a few things."

My neck snaps back. "Under what grounds do you think I have any obligation to answer any of your questions?"

He smirks, happy to answer. "First of all, they're not *my* questions. The district attorney would like to talk to you before he officially charges you with attempted arson. When I saw your name, I was happy to be the one to come down here and get you myself."

"If you're not arresting me, I don't have to go anywhere with you."

"Suit yourself. We were just giving a courtesy to Dean Schumaker. If you need me to take you out of here in handcuffs, I've got the warrant ready to be delivered as soon as I give the word." There's a twinkle of satisfaction in his eye.

He loves this moment. He loves feeling as if he had the upper hand.

Unfortunately, at this moment, he does. I can't possibly allow him to escort me anywhere near campus in handcuffs.

What if someone saw me? It would jeopardize my reputation and therefore my research. Or worse, what if Michelle saw me?

I also need to make sure I won't be riding in the back of a police car.

I'll meet him at the station on my own free will, and I'll wait until my lawyers drop the charges. One good thing my father passed on to me, other than the briefcase, is his flurry of well-appointed and experienced attorneys.

"Fine," I tell him. "I'll see you there." I give him a curt smile before passing by him in my office doorway.

He lets me pass but then follows close behind. "I'm not letting you out of my sight until I see you behind bars, Bishop."

Until now, nobody has ever called me by my last name. When I was young and kept to myself, I noticed all the other kids in middle school and high school would often call each other by their last names. But not me. I figured it was too intimidating since it was linked to my father, but deep down, I knew it was because nobody even called me by my first name. I was a loner nobody spoke to. And, now, I'm on my way to speak to a California district attorney.

"Can I cuff him yet?" Officer Smith asks in his deep voice, directly behind me.

I was greeted by a lawyer from the district attorney's office as well as an investigator as soon as I entered the police station.

"I admire your eagerness." The lawyer slaps the officer on his back. "But we'll take it from here."

Officer Smith sneers under his closed lips.

He hates me. It's obvious. It's almost comforting to know that I'm thought of so much even if it's a less than desirable emotion that I've provoked.

"Let's chat," the same lawyer says to me and gestures for us to walk forward.

"Gentlemen," I say, unaffected by the circumstances, "I'm happy to cooperate with your investigation. But you know as well as I do that my attorneys are on their way. I don't think it would be wise for me to speak with you until they are present."

The investigator leans back on his heels and uses his tongue to make a clicking sound out of the corner of his mouth. "We figured you would have called them by now. Luckily, we have a nice room for you to wait in."

I willfully follow them, knowing I don't have much choice in the matter now that I'm here. Plus, I've only got time on my side until my lawyers show up and shut this whole thing down.

As long as my research and Michelle aren't effected, I really couldn't care less about what happens to me. It's the future of genetic science that would suffer if I were somehow taken out of society.

I would be the one suffering if I were kept from seeing Michelle.

They give me a sandwich and several glasses of water. I have one bathroom break before my attorneys finally enter the room I've been confined to.

"Alexander," a tall man in a long trench coat says as he enters the room.

Another man in a light-gray suit follows behind. I've never met them before, but I know my family is on retainer in case any occasion, such as this, should occur.

I stand up when they enter, but I don't bother to shake their hands. I have no interest in getting to know them.

"Great. Can I go now?" I want to move past them, but they're not giving me the opportunity.

"Not so fast," the tall one says with a looming tone that makes me question my recent sense of freedom. "Should we know how you got that cut on your face?"

I shake my head, and they are happy to turn the other way and pretend it doesn't exist. If I'm not offering information, it's not their problem. At least, not yet.

Our voices bounce off the metal table centered in the room. I glance at the mirror on the wall. I know that our conversations aren't just being recorded; they are being watched from the other side of that glass. The stark whiteness of the floor and ceiling seem blinding now, reflecting the fluorescent light from above.

"What exactly do they have on me?" I ask, sitting back down.

The man in the gray suit taps his finger on the metal table, creating a short echo. "Video surveillance from the Barkers' next-door neighbor's home on December, 24th. They had a camera installed on the inside of their window on their front porch. It catches a man in a brown blazer with similar facial features as you, moving from their porch to the side."

"That's all they've got," the tall attorney pipes in. "They didn't find any fingerprints, and there is only a profile view of the suspect."

I wore those latex gloves, so there wouldn't be any fingerprints. I had my hoodie on under my jacket, so I can't imagine the profile view is incriminating enough for an arrest.

The tall one leans forward. "We need to know your alibi. Once we have that, they'll likely drop the charges. Otherwise, they're looking for an arrest. The district attorney believes they can get a jury to convict based on testimony and the partial profile in the video."

They both sit back and wait for my alibi. I was there, on that porch, and then I slept in my car that night.

"What if I say I was at my apartment alone?" I ask.

The gray suit opens his hands and considers my question. "That would be great. There would be video of you entering your building at a certain time, and we would show that you didn't leave during the time of the attempted crime."

Fuck, that's not going to work.

I glance at the mirror to our side really quick and say, "I don't know for sure right now. I'll have to think and remember where I was that night."

The lawyers nod, understanding what my dilemma is and not wanting to incriminate me further.

The tall one clears his throat. "They're going to want to interview you. We advise you not to answer their questions. Just remain silent, and we'll do all the talking."

I breathe out my stress through my nose, and it makes me think of Michelle—how she often laughs through her nose and how her smile stretches almost across her entire face.

"Of course." I nod to them. I'm beginning to understand I might be in a lot more trouble than I originally thought.

What would this do to my research? I can't just pass along my theories to another genetic scientist and expect him to know how to move forward with it. The design for the pod prototype is all my idea, and the mapping is something only I have been able to prove theories in. I'm the only one who can do this. Whether the world wants me or not, it needs me...and not behind bars.

And what would happen to Michelle? She lives alone; there's nobody out there to make sure she gets home okay at night. There's nobody to make sure Kevin doesn't come around, bothering her again—not that I was any help. But, even if she won't let me near her again, I need to be able to see her.

"Damn it!" I yell and smash my fist on the table, only mildly startling the two gentlemen. "I've been here for almost six hours. When the hell am I going to get to go home?"

"They have a warrant to search your apartment."

A fucking warrant? I can't stand the thought of anyone being in my apartment. That's sacred space, which I have only shared with Michelle. My nostrils flare up in the way I've observed from Michelle in my car, showing my anger.

"They're looking for clothing that matches the suspect on video. Specifically, an identifiable brown blazer."

They won't find any such jacket in my apartment or any other property of mine. Michelle still has my jacket from New Year's Eve. I thought I was protecting her from the chill in the night, but I didn't realize I was also hiding evidence.

"They should have finished the searches by now." The lawyer in the gray suit stands up and buttons his jacket. "They can detain you for up to twenty-four hours without arresting you. I'll go see what's been keeping them and get a feel for whether they're going to follow through with charges."

My jaw cracks when I move it, but I nod.

Before my attorney has a chance to leave the room, the door opens on its own.

One of the lawyers from the district attorney's office walks in, kicking his feet along the way. He sneers at me in such a resentful way that it makes me pull my face back, as if his emotions were physically hitting me.

Why the hell is he looking at me like that?

He looks over to my lawyers. "Your client is a lucky son of a bitch. We were just about to press charges when his alibi walked through the door."

Alibi?

THIRTY-THREE

The lawyer sees the confused expression on my face. "Yes, a young lady, Michelle Stapleton. She says you were with her on the evening of December 24."

The slow intake of air from my gasp feeds my brain with oxygen. *Michelle is giving me an alibi? But why?*

I slowly begin to smile as it hits me that she's giving me an out. I can figure out why later.

"Yes," I say with a full grin, "that's right. That's exactly where I was."

He's holding a manila envelope in his hand, and he slaps it against the other, simultaneously smacking his lips. "I thought you might say that." His eyes shoot daggers, letting me know that he's fully aware that my alibi is false.

"I think we're done here," my tall lawyer says.

I stand up and begin to walk out the door. The district attorney doesn't move as I pass by him.

"I hope you understand how much trouble that girl will be in if we ever find out she's lying for you," he grumbles into my ear. "Interfering with an investigation is a serious crime. If we need to revisit this, we might consider attempted murder versus attempted arson. It's wiser if both of you are honest."

I'll protect her with my life. I might not be able to throw a punch, and I might not be as tough as I'd like, but I can protect her from this. There is no way I would ever let anyone find out about our new little secret. Something that she and I will share.

Her apartment complex doesn't have any video surveillance, and neither do the surrounding buildings. I know because I looked into it recently, but I wore gloves, so there won't be any fingerprints there either.

"My client has been honest," my lawyer jumps in. "Like I said, we're done here." He places his hand on my shoulder and guides me out of the building.

Once we reach the parking lot, I stop my lawyers from moving to their cars. "Would I be putting her at risk if I contacted her?"

They look at each other, having a silent conversation that I'm not a part of.

"Since she's telling the truth," the gray-suit lawyer explains with cautious and telling eyes, "there isn't any harm. *Since* she's telling the truth…"

"I see." I offer my hand, as if I were meeting with someone high up at the university. "Thank you. If you could deal with my accountant for billing, I would appreciate that. There's no need for my father to hear about this."

They seem to understand, and I walk away from them as carefree as if the whole thing never happened.

When I get to my car, I take an overdue deep breath. Michelle came to my rescue.

Why did she do that, and how did she know I needed help?

The police would only know she was lying if they found the jacket. I'll have to contact her. It would be too risky to text or talk over the phone, so I'll have to see her in person even if she doesn't want to see me.

I turn on my car. I plan to drive to the club to cover both my and Michelle's tracks but not before stopping at Michelle's apartment to make sure her lights are on and that she's home.

Knowing she's okay at this very moment is my first priority. Protecting her from any future harm is my second.

I grunt like a bull wanting to charge at something when I see the disarray my office is in. My apartment was one thing but my office. Other than my briefcase transferring paperwork, I've never brought my work home with me. That is a sacred, sterile place for me. Now, I have to live with knowing that multiple hands have scavenged through my personal belongings. The cleaning crew really has its work cut out for them this week.

But this…this truly disturbs me. Papers are creased and sloppily piled in unorganized masses. It wasn't just my car and apartment they were looking for evidence in. Disturbing my work is dangerous to the future of genetic science. I must assume everything is here, just not in the order I need it to be in.

First, I grab my briefcase. I look to the bottom and am relieved to find it hasn't been disturbed. I still have the surveillance devices I used to listen to Penelope in her apartment. I still need these in case Michelle won't see or speak to me again.

Now that I know it's secure, I put my case on the bookshelf and direct my focus on my disaster area of a desk.

I begin to pick up each of the papers sprawled across the surface. My knee kicks at a filing cabinet on the left side that's been left open.

"Ouch!" I yell at my throbbing kneecap after I make contact with my hickory desk.

Angrily, I grab one paper after another until I realize I'm uncovering an object hidden under the research documents. One more sheet comes up and reveals a small glass ball. I can no longer be angry now that I'm thinking about her.

My head snaps and stares at the closed door to my office.

A knock.

I remember what happened last time there was a knock at that door.

Michelle has a class ending soon, and she'll be making her way to her discussion group after that, so I know it's not her on the other side of the door.

Fearing it will be Officer Smith's face I'll see, I hesitate to open. But the knocking continues.

"What?" I hastily say as it swings back violently. "Oh, Dean Schumaker. What can I help you with?"

"Do you have a minute?" he asks.

I flip my wrist over and look at my watch. "I have five." I go back behind my desk, collecting papers.

"What a mess," he observes and reaches down to help me organize.

My hand moves above his in a chopping motion. "No," I say, prompting him to stop touching my papers. "I'm the only one who can make sure it's done properly."

"That's what I came here to talk to you about, Alex."

He takes a seat, but I remain standing, looking from one paper to the other and putting them in the right place.

He folds his leg over his knee and intertwines his fingers on his lap. "Alex, you are very important to this university," he says with intense eyes on me as I move. "There are a lot of things only you can do. I find that it's important to ensure that your final degree comes from Tafford."

"Uh-huh," I mumble as I continue to do what I'm focused on. There's nothing he is saying that I didn't already know.

"You tell me what you need to ensure there are no interruptions in your education here. We are prepared to expel any problems you might have or take on any assets you might need."

I hit a collection of documents on the surface of my desk, making the edges line up properly. But then I stop once I've read between his lines.

"Kevin Durberry…I want him gone," I say sharply to the dean.

"Done."

I soften my tone but try to hold on to my confidence, so he understands it's a demand that cannot be negotiated. "And Michelle Stapleton…I want you to ensure her diploma in psychology at the end of this year. She's a good student, but I want your assurance that, under all circumstances, she will not be denied a degree. She needs to be treated with the same generosity you've shown me."

My thoughts run over Penelope and Nathan. *Do I want Nathan gone? Do I want to give Penelope the same insurance policy I've given Michelle? No, I need to make it clear to Schumaker these two requests are the most important. I don't want to cloud his mind with too many demands.*

"Understood," he says and moves to stand up. "Is that all?"

I wonder if he's thinking that I've missed Nathan Barker's name since it would be public information that his family accused me of attempted arson.

"It's important that you know," he continues, "Tafford is on your side."

He places his hand on my shoulder, as if we had some sort of special relationship. But the relationship we have is one with my research and discoveries and my use for him in situations like this. I know he doesn't really care about me.

"I appreciate that." I move to open the door for him. His five minutes are almost up. "If you don't mind, there's somewhere I need to be."

He nods and leaves my office. Nothing has changed about my understanding of this university's commitment toward me and my research, but now, I can use it to protect Michelle in a way nobody else can.

I take one more glance at the captured poppy on my desk before leaving all my things and heading to the middle of campus.

THIRTY-FOUR

I have Michelle's schedule, so I know where she should be going and what time she should be going there. I wait with my back against a tree in the middle of campus. She needs to cut across the path that runs in the middle of the grand Tafford lawn.

When I look up, I notice the tree is completely bare, and I think about what Michelle told me—how the trees need to let go of the past in order to move along. *Is that what she's doing with me? Is that what I'm doing with Penelope?* I still haven't seen her or stood outside her apartment window since the club. She has Nathan; she doesn't need me anymore. And I have Michelle to fixate on, so I don't need her.

The campus is full of bare trees, but along the outskirts of the university property are tall green trees, still dark and colorful. Evergreens stay green the whole year, hence their name. Maybe there's a way to find a little color in the winter after all. Maybe there's hope for someone like me who can't let anything go, just the same as the evergreens.

I look at my watch and wonder if she's planning to be late or if she decided to take another path to the classroom where she leads her psychology discussion group this semester.

Impatiently, I look around, trying desperately to find some small glimpse of her, but out in the distance, at the very edge of the campus, I see that beautiful strawberry-blonde color I still love. Nothing that's happened takes away from her beauty. It can't be denied.

But Nathan is right there with her. This time, I'm not sneering at the sight of him. His arm is draped around her, and he's giving her more warmth than his body can provide. It's security that he's offering her—in more ways than one. I believe that he'll take care of her in my absence. That's another fact I can't deny. It's possible she might be in better hands.

Twenty minutes go by, and I worry that I won't see Michelle. She's not irresponsible enough to be late for her students.

I need to know where she is. I have to get to my laptop, so I can track her phone.

Turning around to the other side of the tree, with my sights set on the library at the end of the campus park, I stop before I'm able to take more than two steps.

When I lift my head, there she is. Michelle is standing in her khaki peacoat, her caramel-espresso eyes looking straight at me. She adjusts her backpack strap over her shoulder. A nervous habit perhaps, something I take note of.

"That's healing nicely," she says, motioning toward my cheek.

There's a moment of silence where we're just looking at each other.

"I'm really happy to see you," she says, oozing sincerity.

The relief from that small, warm expression takes weight off my shoulders.

My hands go into my pockets because I don't know what else to do with them. "You mean, not in jail? Charges were dropped."

She slowly moves her lips to reveal a smile, but once she realizes that she's about to grin, she purses her lips.

I can't stop staring at her mouth as it moves restlessly, trying to hold back a hint of joy or pride that I've been released. I wish she would kiss me again; even more, I wish I would kiss her. But, right now, I wish my hands weren't in my pockets, and I were touching her somehow. I'm not sure where my boundaries are, so I dig my fists into my jeans, reminding myself to keep them where they are.

"I have so many questions. I feel like I can figure a lot of things out, but I can't figure *you* out. How—why…" I try to think about what I want to ask first. "What are you doing here? Don't you have a discussion group to lead?"

She nods. "I did, but there was a student in my previous group whom I didn't think I should work with. So, I asked the professor if I could switch groups with another aide."

Penelope.

Her name is unsaid, but there's no confusion about what Michelle's eyes are trying to tell me. I didn't obtain Penelope's schedule, so I didn't know.

"How did you know I was in trouble yesterday?"

She licks her bottom lip and becomes more serious. "I found the gloves in your jacket pocket." Leaning into me, so she can lower her voice, she says, "I know you watch *her*, and you've told me she was your obsession, so I knew you must have done something that probably wasn't terribly legal if you needed to use latex gloves for it."

She looks around, making sure there still isn't anyone in earshot. "I wanted to confront you about them, so I went to your office yesterday. The librarian told me that a police officer walked out with you a few minutes before I got there." I wait patiently while she takes a deep breath before continuing, "I..." Her eyes roll around, and she shrugs. "I figured some things out."

"How did you know what day I needed an alibi for?"

Looking at the ground and kicking at the grass, she lifts her head. "I went to the police station and saw someone walk past me with a file that had your name on it. I followed him," she whispers. "When he went into the bathroom, he took the file with him. I was prepared to act like I accidentally went in there, but he had gone into the stall, so I just peeked at the top document and left."

I want to smile and show my pride that she went to such great lengths for me, but I'm torn with detest that she risked so much. My jaw trembles, trying not to tense.

"They're looking for the jacket," I tell her.

"I destroyed it," she quickly says. "They asked me if I'd ever seen you wear anything that would fit its description."

I nod, short and quick movements with my chin, knowing that her destroying my blazer was the best thing for both of us.

"But," she says nervously, "we both wore it at the club on New Year's Eve. That couple saw us in it, so if they look at the video footage, they'll know that I lied and that you really were at that house."

I bring my chin down and look at her through the top of my eyes. I lick my lips before moving to show her a wry smile. "I destroyed it," I say, using her own words.

She leans in even closer and speaks lower, "The club's video footage?"

My head moves up and down. "Yes. After I was released. After I knew you had given me an alibi," I confirm with the same volume of whisper as hers.

She looks up to me, surprised and likely very relieved.

"Michelle, I know I made a fool of myself. But you must know I would never let you get in trouble for what you did for me. I'll do anything."

"No." She shakes her head. "You didn't make a fool of yourself. Just because I ended up needing to think about things doesn't mean you did anything wrong."

She reaches her hand out, as if she wanted to hold mine, but I'm not ready yet. As much as I long for the contact, I know how my obsessions can become overwhelming. Once I have something, I never let it go. I look up to the tree we're under and remember...I guess it's not *never*. I did let go of Penelope.

There's one question I haven't asked yet, and I need to know the answer before I allow myself to touch Michelle again.

THIRTY-FIVE

Michelle's hand relaxes, and she brings it back down by her side when she realizes I'm not going to reach out and hold it.

"Michelle," I begin to ask cautiously and earnestly, "why did you do that for me? Why did you risk your own future to lie for me?" I finally bring one hand out of my pocket and place it gently on my chest. After my point is delivered, I let my hand fall to my side, as Michelle did with hers.

"Because," she speaks with confidence and flings her hair over her shoulder, exposing more of her neck, "I told you, I like to fix people."

There's something about the way she said it that ignites an idea in me. I wonder if she knew about Kevin's philandering ways, and he was just her previous project. Maybe her sadness after the breakup had more to do with her feelings of failure than the reality of his cheating.

But me, I'm fucked up in a very different way.

I shake my head, knowing my ways are set and they can't be repaired. I'm defined by my fixations. "And I told you, I'm obsessive. That can't be *fixed*."

"If you don't think I can fix you, will you at least let me try?" She reaches her hand out for me again.

I feel like she wants the contact as badly as I do.

My eyes lower, and I look at her delicate hand stretched out, reaching for me, and I want it so badly. I want to feel the milky texture of her skin, the soft, tiny hairs near her wrist, and the structure of her bones under her thin flesh.

"I want to touch you." My gaze moves down again, eyeing her hand. "I want to have that, but I'm too afraid you'll take it away once I feel like it's mine."

Her hand moves back down, and I feel like I have my answer. My shoulders slump, and my head feels too heavy to hold high. Suddenly, I feel as tired as I should after too many sleepless nights.

"There's only one thing I can foresee that would make me take it away," she says with reverence. She's small but tough, and her body language is telling me she would go to battle for herself right now. "I don't know if you can choose me over *her*."

Once again, I feel like smiling. I reach my hand out, and she tries not to shudder as the back of my knuckle touches her face. I need to give myself at least this little skin-on-skin contact.

"I already have," I tell her.

I balanced and battled between the feelings I had toward the two women for a couple of weeks, with Michelle growing stronger in my mind every day, but I did choose. When I left that parking lot the other night, I turned left. I chose Michelle.

"You're my new obsession."

Her hand comes up and moves over mine, uncurling my fingers and allowing my entire palm to feel the warmth of her cheeks.

"I think I can live with that," she tells me. "You're my new broken toy."

Her phrasing is a coded message I can understand. We can be each other's bad habits.

Time is our only enemy as it interrupts our much-needed moment together.

"I have to get to class." Her hand is limp next to her left hip, but she opens her palm for me, offering her hand again. "Walk me?" she asks.

I place my hand in hers and begin walking next to her, trying to mimic her steps. I watch her as she looks around, admiring the campus and bare trees, all while knowing exactly where she's going.

We near the psychology hall, and a twinge of pain pricks at me, knowing I'll lose this contact, even for a little bit. It reminds me of nights when I would leave the outside of Penelope's apartment after watching her for hours. But this is so much stronger now that I'm experiencing the touch of my new obsession.

"Oh, shit," Michelle says, prompting me to look straight ahead.

Insecurity and the feelings of being weak and insignificant return. I've taken care of this asshole in the long run, but I want to find some sort of strategic, intellectual way to get rid of him right now. But there's no time, as he's only a few yards in front of us.

"I don't know what to do," I tell Michelle, knowing my own physical limitations.

She squeezes my hand once before releasing it. "Does the university have any cameras directed at us?"

I tell her, "No," excited that she knew I would have a correct answer to that question. I know this campus inside and out and have used their video surveillance system to my advantage in the past. But, right here, in this spot, there's no coverage.

"You just let me take care of it," she says, speeding up her walk.

Kevin focuses on my cheek, the one he made slam into a solid wall, and grins as he steps closer in our direction. "Nice..." he begins to say and raises his arm with one finger pointed out.

Michelle moves, as if she were going to walk right past him, but she grabs his shoulders and shoves her knee between his legs. "Fuck off, Kevin," she says in his ear as she hovers her knee in his crotch, jabbing it just a little harder into him before bringing it down.

My groin aches, subliminally feeling Kevin's pain and partially because I'm turned on by Michelle's self-assurance and aggressiveness. I can learn more than just social cues from this woman.

His face is instantly beet red, and when Michelle moves from between his legs, he collapses to the ground with a moan that would make a circling predatory bird assume he's dying.

He mumbles something through the pain that sounds like, "Bitch."

Michelle bends down and says, "If you come near either of us again, I'll say you attacked me."

I want to celebrate for her. I've never been so proud of anyone, not even Penelope.

Michelle backtracks a few steps to once again hold my hand. Stunned and impressed, I'm eager to give it to her. I'm eager to know where we will go with this physically because I'm really turned on.

In a way, she'll be my first—not literally, but the first time I haven't paid for it—and I have a feeling she'll love that fact.

We walk past Kevin's pained body and bruised ego, as if he were nothing.

There isn't much farther to go, but I make sure to walk her all the way to the psychology building.

"I think you and I could make a great team," Michelle says before rising on her toes to give me an innocent kiss on the cheek. Only it's not innocent to me, but she knows that.

"I was just thinking the same thing," I whisper in her ear before she pulls away from my face.

Her smile tells me everything I need to know about our future together. I tug at her arm. "You know, you don't actually have to go to class. You and I can do whatever we want."

She tilts her head. "What do you mean?"

I feel my grin slowly grow across my face. "I've guaranteed your master's degree."

She breathes in sharp and straightens her body as she smiles.

"So, what do you want to do?"

Her eyes flicker up and down my body. "We've got all day. Let's go people-watching."

If what Michelle says is true—that our worst trait is also our best—then I can only assume that theory applies to our relationships. If Michelle is the best thing in my life, she might also be the worst.

But what the fuck do I care? I'm Alexander George Bishop V, and I can get away with anything.

THANK YOU

I'm not exaggerating when I say, I would not be an author if it wasn't for Sara Blanchard.

I had this urge to write a story. It was something I started but wasn't feeling confident enough to follow through and publish. I didn't know I was an author yet. But, at the perfect time to catapult my ambitions and become a novelist, Sara moved next door. She became my cheerleader and encouraged me through moments of doubt and insecurity. Little did I know, she had so much more to bring into my life.

We quickly became friends. But, naive little me, I thought she was just another stay-at-home/working mom like me.

You know the moms who *need* more, the ones who are stay-at-home moms and primary caregivers but also have the need to work and contribute to the adult community? That's me.

I finished my first novel with her holding my hand through the entire process. I felt like an author, but I still struggled with the balancing act of being a mom and wife. With love and encouragement, Sara imparted her wisdom on me. She told me about *Flex Mom*, her debut non-fiction book about the third category of momhood.

If it wasn't for *Flex Mom*, I wouldn't have found a way to do it all. I'm still a stay-at-home mom, but I have a full-time career as a storyteller.

She is still the first person who reads every story I write. I love her criticism because it comes from such a sincere and constructive place, as if we had the same goal for my novels.

If I haven't been able to express it yet, Sara, you are invaluable to me. You are a treasure that walked into my life at the perfect moment. From the bottom of my heart, thank you.

Sara isn't the only amazing and inspiring woman in my life. I live in a community full of them!

Thank you to Sarah Stabio at Bar Method. You have provided me and our neighborhood with a place to gain strength, see friends, and enjoy working out. Your studio has made a big difference in my life and brought me so much inspiration.

I have found an incredible support system in the Conservatory Green Book Club—my new go-to place for beta readers. It's hard to put yourself out there, but the welcome and encouragement I get from these women make me feel strong and confident. Thank you for all your feedback and support.

I've made so many invaluable friends during the past couple of years.

Marguerite, you have given me a type of friendship I didn't know I could have again after becoming a mother. I love how I can isolate myself in my family life but then yell to my husband after the kids go to bed, "I'm going to my friend's house." You have become such an important friend to me. Thank you for supporting me, laughing with me— sometimes at me—and drinking wine with me.

I couldn't make it through a day without my daily phone call with my dad and sister-in-law. Thank you for letting me share EVERYTHING with you and for never screening my calls. I wouldn't blame you if you did.

This year has been absolutely crazy! My creative juices have been flowing, and I've been so focused on writing. The hard part about that is choosing which project to move forward with first.

Luckily, I have the most wonderful editors—Madison Seidler and Jovana Shirley. Thank you for being flexible, honest, and dedicated. It has made such a difference in my writing and sanity to know I have such an incredible and compassionate team behind me.

Lauren, James, and Dash—You are family I got to choose. Your friendship and support have remained constant and unwavering. It's a rock at the base of my life. I know you will always be there for me. I only hope you feel the same love from me that you have given to my family.

Autumn Gantz, you are incredible! I honestly don't know what I did before we met. I'm so looking forward to working with you for a long time. Thank you!

It's no secret, I'm madly in love with my husband. It's something I shout from the rooftops every chance I get. Although I'm not a psychopath like Alex, I'm just as obsessive. I have the most incredible life because of all the hard work my husband puts into choosing happiness with me. I've never felt so fulfilled as I do from being able to write.

Phil, you are the center of all that I do. I love you with all my heart...and so much more.

ABOUT THE AUTHOR

Erin Lockwood grew up in Castro Valley, California, and attended the University of Oregon where she graduated with a degree in journalism in 2003. From there, she moved to Denver, Colorado, and spent the next seven years searching for the love of her life and then building the family of her dreams.

It wasn't long until, with children starting preschool and more time on her hands, Erin refocused on her career, beginning with a successful entry into the world of residential real estate as a realtor. Free time was spent reading book after book—and binge-watching the subsequent films—in the New Adult genre. Hopelessly in love with her husband, she wrote him a short story for their wedding anniversary. That was when she discovered her tireless passion to tell stories.

Erin still lives in Denver with her husband, Phil, and their three children. They spend most of their summers and holidays on the beautiful island of Coronado where Erin and Phil wish to retire someday.

Learn more about Erin and other novels at www.erinlockwood.com, www.facebook.com/erinlockwoodauthor, and http://twitter.com/elockwoodbooks.

Made in the USA
San Bernardino, CA
03 July 2017